Prelude of a Guardian Angel

Ben Logsdon

Copyright © 2024 by Benjamin Logsdon

Prelude of a Guardian Angel is a work of fiction. Names, places, characters, and incidents are either the product of the author's imagination or are used fictitiously. Any resemblance to actual persons, living or dead, events, or locales is entirely coincidental.

All rights reserved. No part of this publication may be reproduced, distributed, or transmitted in any form or by any means, including photocopying, recording, or other electronic or mechanical methods, except for the use of quotations in a book review, without the prior written permission of the copyright holder.

First edition 2024

ISBN: 979-8-218-54820-9 (paperback)

ASIN: B0D9J96HYX (digital)

Cover by Carmella Grace

Instagram: @rednovabooks

TikTok: @rednovabooks

Twitter/X: @Ben_Logsdon_363

Published by Red Nova Books LLC

Contents

Dedication	VIII
1. First Class	1
2. The Dawn of Wrath	18
3. Judge and Jury	39
4. Sanctuary Lost	51
5. The Rendezvous Point	73
6. Homecoming	98
7. The Greatest Teacher	110
Afterword	130
Acknowledgments	131
About The Author	133

To my wife and children—
my own little Heaven on Earth.

Chapter 1
First Class

HIGH SCHOOL IS OF THE DEVIL. That's what all the other angels kept telling me. I didn't believe them at first. Elementary was a breeze for Daniela. Middle school, too. She was always such a bright and sociable little girl. What was the worst that could happen by throwing some extra hormones and a smidge of peer pressure into the mix?

Granted, her freshman year was quite the doozy. Braces, growth spurts, and after moving to the city of Upland, starting from scratch in the friends department. The poor thing was a metal-mouthed deer in the headlights, but as her grandmother and sworn guardian, I wasn't about to let Dani go down without a fight. No matter how feral or degenerate the other kids were, I made sure to keep her chin held high, focusing the bulk of her teenage angst toward her studies. She eventually met Bonnie, and from then on, they were a force of nature. The darkness of the world couldn't touch them. At least, not while they were together.

Things would be different now. Today would mark the beginning of a new and perilous journey. Our last, lonely pilgrimage into an unholy land. A place bereft of all hope and reason, consumed by a virulent chaos the peoples of antiquity could never have fathomed...

Keystone High.

"Did you remember to grab the lunch bag I packed for you?" Daniela's mom, Carmen, tapped the steering wheel of their Chevy Astro van, her eyes flitting between the passenger seat and the morning traffic. "There should be a couple of fresh empanadas inside. You still like the ones with ham in them, don't you?"

Dani nodded beside her, wistfully gazing out the window.

"Listen, I...I know it isn't going to be the same without Bonnie," Carmen sighed. "You'll have to get out of your comfort zone a little bit, but things will work out. You'll see."

"Why did she have to move away right before our senior year?" Dani grumbled. "This was supposed to be our moment of triumph. Class of 2005. What's so great about crappy old Virginia anyway?"

Carmen shrugged her shoulders. "Not every parent gets to choose where their job is," she replied. "Bonnie's dad would've loved to stay in California, but his company changed their HQ. You can't expect him to simply up and quit for the sake of you and your bestie."

"Sure I can," Dani said, folding her arms in disdain.

I sat behind them next to Carmen's angel, Laila, soaking up the awkward silence that followed. It wasn't like Dani to whine so childishly. The entitlement in her voice made me want to reach through the back of her chair and invisibly slap her upside the head.

"Calm down, Sarai," Laila said with a grin. "Even with your mouth closed, I can tell when you're grinding your teeth. It's totally natural for a kid to be stressed on the first day of school. Cut her some slack for once."

I relaxed my jaw, taking a moment to gather my faculties. "Yeah...yeah, you're right. We've done this a dozen times before. We can do it again."

"That's the spirit, chica." Laila playfully whipped me in the leg with her long braid of russet brown hair, knocking away my worries in an instant. She always had a talent for that sort of thing, trivializing the disasters in my mind with a single act of kind-hearted mischief. It was a wisdom that even several decades of mortality had failed to teach me. To think hers lasted only a few hours, cut tragically short by a congenital lung defect, yet here she was, mentoring me as though I'd left my body only yesterday.

"If you smack me with that thing one more time, I'm gonna chop it off," I said, chuckling.

"You wouldn't dare!" She tucked the braid behind herself, feigning surprise. "You're just jealous because you can't weaponize that lame half-up, half-down bun of yours."

"Guilty as charged," I said, rolling my eyes. "If only I had a giant tassel attached to my head. The diablos would run screaming at my awesome power."

"Maybe it's the reason Scarvin usually decides to stay home," Laila retorted. "Who knows? It might even explain why Gigglewarts got re-assigned."

I shot the angel a skeptical look. "None of those dregs down in Inferno are scared of your hairstyle, Laila. They probably figured Giggles wasn't making any progress with Dani and sent him to corrupt an easier target."

"You think they'll assign her a new demon?" Laila asked, stroking her chin. "It's been almost a week and still no replacement. I wonder if they're planning to have Scarvin cover the whole family by himself."

"One can only hope." I adjusted the sash of my snowy white robes, the paranoia catching back up with me. "What if the diablitos have something more nefarious in store? They could have an ambush waiting at the school." I straightened in my chair, a thousand crazy scenarios flooding my imagination. "What if Dani gets there and joins a death cult? Without Bonnie, who would talk her out of it? She could end up addicted to hip hop music and booty shorts! And what about social media? They could push her to get piercings on her—"

"*Cálmate, loca!*" Laila whipped her braid again, slapping me across the face.

The shock of it set me off like a powder keg. I instinctively lunged at my assailant, reaching to grab her by the hair, but she was one step ahead of me.

She gently snatched my hand, a patient smile on her face, those big brown eyes peering straight into mine. "It's gonna be fine, Sarai. Dani's a good girl. You've worked hard to keep her that way since she was five years old, but you can't shelter her forever. It's her life. Her choices. Have some faith in her, okay? Have some faith in yourself."

The words hit me so much harder than her strike to the face. She was right. I wanted to believe my promptings were in Dani's best interest, but it wasn't love that was compelling me. It was fear.

I shrank back into my seat, glancing down at the floor. "I...I'm sorry, Laila. I just want to protect her."

The angel gave my hand a reassuring squeeze. "And you will. The Rivera family always takes care of its own."

"Here we are!" Carmen said, pulling over to the school's drop-off area. She tried to inject a bit of enthusiasm in her voice, but Dani simply pursed her lips. "Have fun and hang out with some of the smart kids. It might come in handy if you have to do any group projects."

"Yeah, yeah." Dani pushed open the passenger door, slinging her backpack over her shoulder. "See you after school."

"Love you!" Carmen said as Dani went to close the door.

The teenager froze for a moment, looking around to see if any of the other new arrivals had overheard. A hint of embarrassment? It was always a mystery to me why such a basic human expression would be a social taboo.

I leaned forward between the front seats, projecting my influence on Daniela. "Answer your mother, mi amor. She was nice enough to drive you all the way here."

Dani's face quickly softened. "Love you too, Mom."

"That's my girl."

Dani shut the door with a wave, Carmen taking a few extra seconds to watch her disappear into the growing crowd of students.

"Welp, guess that's my cue," I said, turning to Laila.

She flashed an encouraging smile, snagging me by the hem of my robe. "If you want me to, I can tag along and help out. I'm sure Carmen will survive a few hours at work without me."

I graciously shook my head. "Thanks, but I haven't needed help since the day I died. Don't worry, amiga. I've got this."

I levitated out of my seat and passed through the side of the van, emerging into the noisy bustle of the school's entrance. Kids herded along in the morning sunlight, checking their maps and schedules, some congregating beneath the maple trees of the campus front lawn. They came in so many shapes and sizes, each blissfully unaware of the corresponding spirits trailing behind them. Demons hovered over every shoulder, a twisted shadow of the angels they once were, whispering fears and temptations while their heavenly counterparts gave words of encouragement. I spotted Dani heading for the main gate, stepping forward in pursuit when a familiar voice caught my attention.

"Sarai? Sarai, is that you?" A slender angel with baby-blue eyes and silvery long hair came running up beside me, smiling and breathless. "It's me, Ariel, from last year's English class, remember?"

"How could I forget?" I said politely.

In truth, I really couldn't. She'd spent every waking minute of Dani's third period blabbing to me about her mortal's eccentricities. Eating habits. Bowel movements. Favorite comic books and movies. The former human in me wished I could've simply told her to shut her trap and focus on her charge's behavior, but of course, the divinity in me wouldn't have it. Instead, I let my eyes glaze over and pretended to listen, trying not to let her distract me from the task at hand. It seemed this year would be more of the same.

"You know, I'd love to stick around and chat, but my human is wandering off and I really need to—"

"Not a problem!" Ariel interjected. "We can find her together! Come on!" She grabbed me by the arm, leading me onto the front lawn without missing a beat. "Have I ever told you how fabulous you look?"

"You may have mentioned it once or twice," I said with a blank expression.

"I *mean* it, though. That perfect raven hair, those high cheekbones, oh, and that flawless copper skin! It's absolutely to *live* for! One day, when I finally get to be born, you think my mortal body will ever be as gorgeous as you?"

"If you eat your vegetables and get plenty of exercise..."

"I know, right? They say physical bodies take a *lot* of work, what with all the breathing and the digestion. Tell me, what was it like to have ice cream? Does it really freeze your brain?"

"Ariel, could you stop badgering the poor girl? She just wants to get from A to B without the Spanish Inquisition." Another angel strolled up beside us, gesturing for Ariel to release my arm. He was a tad shorter than me, rosy-cheeked and portly with a quiff of sandy blond hair.

"Hey, Javan," I said, grateful for the intervention.

He gave me a wink, nudging me with his elbow. "Unborns, am I right?"

"Y-yeah...they're pretty excitable." I sheepishly rubbed the back of my neck, glancing around for a change of subject. Dani had taken a detour just inside the main gate, pausing to speak with a couple of girls in dangerously short skirts. "*Ay, bendito!* Can you believe the kids these days? It's like they're all in a contest to see who can show up to school with the least amount of clothing. When I was a teenager, we had to wear dresses down to the knee."

Ariel narrowed her eyes. "Wasn't that back in the 1940's or something?"

"Heh, we didn't even *have* schools in ancient Jericho," Javan snorted. "Then again, maybe that's why we were so horrible at building walls..."

"It doesn't matter what time period I'm from," I replied. "A person's beauty shouldn't be measured by how much skin they're showing. Aren't either of you concerned about all the negative influences around here?"

The two angels exchanged looks.

"Maybe a little bit," Javan shrugged, "but have you seen what we're dealing with? These pups are barely house-trained. Even if we could hogtie them to their parents' couch, they'd still have TV and internet. Temptations are everywhere. I count myself lucky that my boy, Alex, has his nose permanently glued to that video game thingamajig he carries around. Could be doing a lot worse."

"My girl, Corinne, is too busy reading to get into any trouble," Ariel chipped in.

"Really? What kind of stuff does she read?" I asked.

"Mostly magazines with shirtless men on them, but I doubt her demon will get too much mileage out of something like that."

I buried my face in my hand, teeth grinding in frustration. "Have you guys tried spending more time with your mortals instead of socializing? It might help keep their diablitos in check. You could even collaborate with their parents' angels to make sure someone teaches them proper behavior."

Javan raised an eyebrow. "Is that last one still an option?"

"I'm not so sure," Ariel said, wringing the frills of her shiny white dress. "The parents seem to really have their hands full tinkering with their iPods and watching reality TV shows. You think we could squeeze in a few minutes before bed?"

I stared at the two of them with eyes wide, fighting back the urge to explode when the droning of a bell sounded over the school's PA system. Finally, a means of escape. Dani broke away from the girls she was talking to and hurried through the inner courtyard, disappearing into the stairwell of the farthest classroom building.

"Sorry, guys, gotta run! Don't want to be late for first period!" I tossed the angels a half-hearted wave and pushed off the ground, launching myself through the air after my granddaughter.

It was so freeing to feel the wind on my face, in my hair, nothing left to get between me and my mission. Through the second-story windows, I could see Dani eyeballing the numbers of each classroom door, ducking into one labeled "236." With a tilt of my arms, I altered my trajectory, gliding through the solid glass window pane into the building's open hallway. I somersaulted to stick the landing, graceful as a gymnast, casually dusting off my robes before strolling through the classroom door.

The din of laughter and shifting desks immediately assaulted my ears, students chattering amongst themselves while their accompanying spirits stood over them. Dani was settling into a chair by the window, her backpack resting at her feet as she looked around for anybody she recognized. Most of the room was packed with fresh faces, though I managed to spy a few familiar ones mixed into the crowd.

There was Brianna and Scott, the jokesters from last year's history class, both snickering in the front row as their angels greeted me with a wave. Loraine from sophomore geometry was always a delight. She locked eyes with my granddaughter from the second row, the two acknowledging each other with a grin. But that demon of hers. I couldn't remember his name, but he just kept pointing at me with the same menacing glower. Apparently, he hadn't forgotten the time I punched him in the throat for making too many lewd hand gestures.

Beside Dani sat a boy with bushy eyebrows and spiky black hair, drumming the top of his desk with a pair of unsharpened pencils. He seemed to lose himself in a rhythm only he could hear, closing his eyes as he pounded his imaginary cymbals. Dani didn't really pay him any mind, but I was shrewd enough to see it. The subtle glances he was throwing her.

That filthy little hedgehog was trying to flirt! Not on *my* watch, perro. No grandchild of mine would be caught associating with such a juvenile delinquent. I stormed across the classroom to Dani's side, tapping the boy's angel on the shoulder to reprimand him for his flagrant negligence.

"Oi, could you do me a favor and keep your punk's eyes to himsehhh..." My voice trailed off as the angel turned around, flashing me the most incredible smile.

In all my years, both living and dead, I'd seen my fair share of attractive men. Tall, dark, with just the right amount of stubble on their chin. This guy put them all to shame. His physique was slim yet toned, his bare arms and chest rippling from his sleeveless tunic. He ran a hand through his short feathery brown hair, meeting my gaze with eyes as deep and sparkly as emeralds.

"Forgive me, Milady," he said, bowing ever so slightly. "Has my charge done something to offend you?"

"I, uh...well, I...um...he, uh..."

"Of course. Where are my manners?" The angel extended his hand in greeting. "I'm Ethan."

I reached out to give him a shake, my face contorting into a goofy smile. "Sarai."

"Ah, what a lovely name. It's truly an honor to meet you, Sarai."

I expected him to simply grip my hand with a quick bob like any other normal person, but instead he raised it to his lips, gracing my knuckles with an elegant kiss. A tingle of embarrassment shot up my arm into my body, turning my face red as a tomato.

"Th-that's not really necessary," I said, gently pulling my hand away.

Ethan grinned wider, wrinkling his forehead. "My apologies. As a former Knight of the Templar, the ways of classical chivalry are deeply ingrained in me."

"Old habits die hard, huh?"

"I suppose there's some truth to that. Now then, what act of malfeasance has my charge committed against yours?"

"Oh, it really wasn't that big of a deal," I said, waving my hand dismissively. "I just noticed him trying to impress my girl and wanted to make sure things didn't get out of control."

Ethan deflated a little. "Yes, I see. Keeping his thoughts free of carnal desire is an ever-daunting task when his demon is around..." He stepped to the side, revealing the spirit standing opposite his human boy.

I recoiled in disgust, gawking at the particularly vile succubus. She reminded me of the evil phantom girl from a horror movie Dani had once watched while her parents were out of town. The one with veiny, pale blue skin and a grungy mop of hair hanging down over her face. I think the character lived in a well or something, occasionally climbing out of TV screens to scare people to death. Anyway, this demon was the spitting image, clear down to the ragged nightgown and the one sinisterly visible eye.

She gave me a spiteful sideways glance, hissing with the same level of revulsion. "Piss off, Pocahontas."

"*Pocahontas?* I'm from Puerto Rico, you uncultured hag!" I lurched forward, fists clenched and ready to fly when Ethan moved between us.

"Ladies! Ladies! Please, let's take a moment and show some civility."

"She started it!" I said, glaring over his shoulder.

"*You're* the one throwing around false accusations!" the demon shot back. "Why would my human be interested in your goody-goody-two-shoes nerd over there? I've been pointing him at the jackpot all morning." The succubus nodded to a pretty blonde girl sitting in front of the drummer boy. She was surrounded by a fan club of other students, captivating them with her every word and gesture.

"It's true," Ethan agreed. "Jezazel may be a foul creature, but she's never been shy about confessing her real intentions."

"Is that so?" I backed away with a sigh, relieved to hear Daniela wasn't a target, yet still a bit perturbed to see an angel siding with his dark counterpart.

Over by the popular blonde girl, another succubus began eyeing us suspiciously. This one was much more voluptuous than Jezazel, wearing a skimpy cocktail dress fashioned from what appeared to be human skin. Her long mane of cerulean hair flickered and glowed down her back, dancing in a single uninterrupted flame.

"Hey, Jez, what's the hold-up?" she barked at Ethan's demon. "I went through all the trouble of getting my girl into this expensive designer outfit and your human hasn't even joined the groupies yet. I thought you said he was into her."

"Give me a break, Diva," Jezazel croaked in reply. "You know how fickle these kids can be. It doesn't help with these featherbacks getting in the way either." She jabbed a grimy thumb in my direction. "Princess Prude here is trying to distract us with her brat's innocent farmgirl routine."

"We were doing nothing of the sort!" I gasped. "Dani's been minding her own business waiting for class to start."

"Oh yeah? Then what do you call that?" Jezazel pointed down at Ethan's waist, the two of us only now realizing that his boy was leaning through his ghostly torso with a playful smirk.

"How's it goin'?" the drummer said to Dani. "The name's Hector. Hector Torres. I guess we're gonna be neighbors this year?"

"It sure looks that way," Dani said, bashfully twirling her ponytail.

"I think I've seen you somewhere before," Hector mused. "You were in the school choir last year, weren't you?"

Dani slowly nodded, squinting as she tried to recall ever seeing him. "Yeah...yeah, I was, but how did you—?"

"The marching band shares a door with the choir room. A few of us were going to do some after-school practicing when we heard you guys singing. You've got a rockin' set of pipes, by the way."

Dani glanced down at her desk, cheeks burning. "Th-thanks..."

"I'm captain of the drumline in case you were wondering. Got my own quad set and everything."

"I figured as much," Dani chuckled. "That was a pretty crazy show you were putting on just now."

Hector smugly cracked his knuckles. "Yep, sometimes the music just comes to me and I gotta go with the flow. You ever feel that way...uh...?" He spun his finger in front of him, pretending to search for a name my granddaughter had yet to give.

"Oh, sorry. I'm Dani. Dani Rivera."

Another voice suddenly cut between them, silky and smooth as velvet. "Nice to meet you, Dani! I'm Candace!" The blonde girl from earlier had shifted around in her seat, her cherry lips pulled into a dimpled smile. "Are you planning to join any clubs this year? The debate team could use some more fresh blood."

"I haven't really thought about it," Dani admitted. "I take it you're a member?"

Candace flipped her hair with a giggle, feigning humility. "Oh gosh, our coach may or may not have made me the president."

"Come on," Hector shrugged. "Debate is all you ever talk about. Aren't you like a world-class champion or something?"

She paused for a moment, unable to resist the opportunity to boast. "Citrus Belt Regional Tournament winner three years running, but whatevs. I just love discussing ideas with people, mulling over all the important issues. One day, I hope to go to the same law school as my dad."

"Wow, a family of lawyers?" Jezazel chimed in. "How'd you get a sweet setup like that, Diva?"

Candace's demon flashed a toothy grin. "'Follow the money,' babe. That's my motto."

Hector slouched back in his chair, oblivious to the spiritual commentary. "Look at this over-achiever, already shooting for Harvard."

"You've got to aim high if you want to make it in life," Candace retorted. "Everything's a competition whether people admit it or not. Getting into college? Getting a career? The kind of friends we can make?" She leaned over to Dani, lowering her voice, a mischievous smile tugging at the corners of her mouth. "It's not enough to simply strive for greatness. You have to surround yourself with it. You have to look the part." Her crystal-blue eyes flicked over Dani's shoulder. "You don't want the boat anchors of society weighing you down."

The rest of us turned to follow Candace's gaze, spotting a girl sitting by herself in the corner. She already had an open notebook and pencil laid across the desk in front of her, quietly waiting for the teacher to arrive. An admirable gesture as far as I was concerned, but there was definitely something about her appearance that struck me as odd. She wasn't wearing even a hint of makeup, exposing a complexion riddled with scars and acne. Her wavy chestnut hair was tied back in a pair of uneven pigtails, each bound with a green ribbon to match her simple long-sleeved dress.

"Check out that dumpster fire of an outfit," Candace jeered. "Was it sewn by hand? I didn't realize nuns could wear color." The other girls in her fan club erupted into laughter. Dani folded her arms, nervously hiding her *Lord of the Rings* T-shirt from Candace's fashion-minded vitriol. "It looks like some people are gearing up to graduate right onto skid row."

I shook my head, turning to the other spirits. "What a vulgar little bruja."

"I know. Isn't she the best?" Diva said proudly.

"What the heaven is a 'bruja'?" Jezazel asked, scratching her head.

Ethan and I exchanged grins. "It means 'witch' in Spanish," he replied.

"You should already be an expert on the subject," I said to Jezazel.

"What did you say?" Her hands tensed at her sides, their gnarled fingernails beginning to extend into claws when the classroom door flung open behind her.

"Alright, everybody, settle down!" The teacher's voice jolted everyone to attention, students and spirits alike. He adjusted his thick, black-rimmed glasses, surveying the latest crop of fresh young minds. "Welcome back to Keystone High, ladies and gents. I'm Mr. Elliot and I'll be your guide through the whimsical world of macroeconomics. Now then, let's see if I can find the roll sheet..." He laced his fingers over his big round belly, sauntering to the podium while the class broke out their books and writing supplies.

The angels and demons in the room returned to their assigned mortals, hunkering down for the boring lecture to come. I wasn't exactly thrilled at the prospect after having lived through the entire grade school experience once before, but at least the distraction would keep Dani out of trouble for a spell. It gave me time to plan how we would navigate the social minefield of teenage politics. What alliances needed to be made? Which enemies were waiting to stab us in the back? There were so many paths to catastrophe, a single wrong move threatening to turn us into a victim or a pariah, but how would that be different from any other day?

I was a protector of souls, and this battle was just getting started.

Chapter 2

THE DAWN OF WRATH

THE REST OF DANI'S morning classes went as smoothly as one could expect. English, Chemistry and then a dash of AP Physics. It was a good thing she was a lot smarter than I was at her age. Half the stuff these modern kids were learning would've made my tiny little head explode, but she took it like a champ. Nothing could break her stride. That is, not until lunchtime rolled around.

You'd think the whole ritual would be simple enough. Sit down, eat your food, maybe chat with some friends for a bit, then move on to the next scholastic endeavor. But nope. Not in the human world. The moment Dani strolled into the cafeteria, the 4D chess was already in play.

She glanced around the cavernous room, trying to decide where to sit down with the sack lunch her mama had made for her. Almost all the tables were brimming with students, each representing different factions of the social hierarchy. There were the jocks and the band geeks, skaters and bookworms. As far as I could tell, Dani never felt any attachment to a particular group. Her pleasant demeanor and reasonably good looks had always allowed her to mingle seamlessly with whomever she wanted. But where did she *belong?* The only person that ever made her feel that way was Bonnie. Without her, the room might as well have been empty.

"Hey, Dani! Over here!" A few tables down, Hector was waving his arm in the air, beckoning for her to come sit. He was flanked by Candace and several members of her entourage, their accompanying spirits huddled around them as well. I recognized Ethan, Jezazel and Diva, not to mention a couple of angels that had ventured away from their humans yet again.

"Sarai! Come and join us!" Ariel shouted, jumping up and down next to Javan.

I leaned close to Dani, whispering in her ear. "You should go sit with the bookworms over by the vending machine, mi amor. Maybe you guys could throw together a study group?"

Dani paused, taking a moment to consider the words drifting through her subconscious, then dismissed them with a subtle shake of her head and shuffled towards the drummer boy.

"W-wait! You don't want to go over there," I hissed, ducking behind her. "It'd be much better to hang out with the honor students, not some punk rocker and his evil Barbie doll."

But it was no use. Dani ignored my promptings, smiling as she approached Hector's table. "Got room for one more?" she asked.

"Always," Hector said, making space between himself and Candace. Dani plopped down onto the bench, pulling open her sack lunch while the other angels swarmed around us.

"Hey, girl, how ya been?" Ariel squealed, throwing her arms around me. "For a minute there, I was worried your mortal was going to sit on the other side of the room."

"Perish the thought," I muttered, standing stiff as a board.

She sprang backward and clutched my hands, totally unfazed by my intended sarcasm. "Tell us all about your day. Have you guys made any new friends? Learned anything cool? Oh, and what about your teachers? Do they scream in the kids' faces too?"

"The teachers are downright savage this year," Javan added with a pout. "Alex got his video game thingy confiscated in the first five minutes, and he wasn't even playing with the sound on."

"How devastating," I said flatly.

"Right? The poor lad is already suffering from withdrawals!"

Ethan inched up and grabbed Javan by the shoulders, pacifying him with a lighthearted jostle. "Relax, my friend. I'm sure your mortal will find a way to survive." Ethan fixed his piercing green eyes on me, robbing my legs of their strength for a split-second. "It's good to see you again, Milady."

"Uh, y-yeah..." I gently tugged my hands free of Ariel's grip, straightening my posture. "You really don't need to call me that, you know. It's not like I'm royalty or anything."

"I beg to differ," Ethan replied. "The Father considers all of His daughters royalty, Milady. Why should I not treat them in kind?"

"What a steaming load of horse crap," Jezazel croaked from behind him. "I was created the same as her once, but you've never thrown around any of those groveling titles with *me*."

Ethan glared over his shoulder. "That's because you reduced yourself to a soul-sucking harpy by joining Lucifer's rebellion against the Father."

"Oh, please. You're just a brown-nosing parasite trying to flatter your way into somebody's robes."

Ethan's jaw dropped, his brows twitching with indignation. "W-w-*wuh?* You perverse little goblin! How dare you make such obscene accusations! I would never impugn the virtue of another divine being. I address all of my cohorts with equal respect."

Jezazel cocked her head. "Really? Who else do you call 'Milady'?"

All the surrounding female angels raised their hands.

"Oh…"

I leaned forward with a smug grin. "Is that a hint of jealousy I detect, bruja?"

Hector's voice abruptly cut in beside us. "Whoa, that's one heck of a lunch you got there."

While we spirits were talking, Dani had laid out the contents of her bag on the table. There was a bundle of mouthwatering empanadas wrapped in paper towels, the scent of beef, ham and chicken blossoming from within. A plastic bowl of rice, beans and sweet potato cubes glistened alongside them, complemented by a carton of chocolate milk. Hector glanced between the feast and his soggy peanut butter and jelly sandwich, wiping the drool from his chin.

"You think I could try a piece of empanada?" he pleaded.

"Of course," Dani said, handing him one of the pastries.

He greedily stuffed it in his mouth, moaning in ecstasy as Candace stared with her eyes wide.

"Geez, Hector, you and that burrito should probably get a room," she sneered.

"It's not actually a burrito," Dani corrected. "Those are made from—"

"Yeah, yeah, very fascinating," Candace interrupted. "I'm sure your mommy does a great job packing your lunch for you." She turned to her tray of cafeteria lasagna, poking it with her spork. "I've always been a bigger fan of Italian food anyway."

"Me too," Dani said, forcing a smile. "My mom helps me out when she has the chance, but I'm the one that usually does most of the cooking at home."

Candace furrowed her brow. "Your mom makes you do it?"

Dani shook her head. "Not at all. I love to cook and experiment with new recipes. My dream is to go to Le Cordon Bleu College of Culinary Arts in L.A. and become a professional chef."

"No way," Hector said, swallowing the last of his empanada. "That's hardcore."

"I've been studying international cuisine since I was eight years old. Lasagna happens to be one of my specialties. If you want, Candace, I could whip up a batch later this week for us to share."

"Thanks, but maybe you should save your charity for the poor," Candace replied. "I bet Pigtails over there would die for something that wasn't dug out of the garbage." She pointed her spork at a table on the farthest side of the room. Its benches were completely vacant save for a lone girl. The one from first period with the shabby long-sleeved dress.

She sat quietly hunched over a bowl of salad, eyes down, struggling to ignore the barrage of scornful looks coming from the surrounding tables. I hadn't noticed him before, but her angel was standing out in front of her now, shielding her from the unheard jeers and heckling of her tormentors' demons. It was painful to see him there, sword drawn, shouting at the devils to stay back as a growing crowd clawed at his robes and curly orange hair.

Meanwhile, the girl's personal tempter was perched on her shoulder, small and monkeylike with freakishly bulbous eyes and a bladed tail. He leaned close, hand cupped to his mouth, no doubt whispering words of discouragement and self-loathing in her ear.

"Who is she?" Dani finally asked.

"I think Mr. Elliot said her name was Beth Starkovsky," Hector whispered. "According to the guys in my programming class, she's pretty weird. Spent her whole life getting homeschooled and decided to slum it with us common folk for her senior year. They say she dresses like that because her parents are super religious or something."

"And nobody wants to sit with her?"

"You're welcome to be the first," Candace shrugged. "Just make sure you've had all your shots. Wouldn't want to catch rabies."

I folded my arms, gazing sympathetically at the besieged girl and her angel. "Somebody needs to bring a dose of compassion to this petty madness. Maybe Dani *should* be the one to do it."

"Careful," Javan warned. "None of us enjoy watching someone get bullied, but if you put your mortal between the wolves and their prey, it's only going to give them a larger meal."

"He's right," Ariel squeaked. "Dani was lucky enough to get a seat at the popular table. If you push her to sit with that outcast, she'll end up as one too."

I gaped at both of them, utterly appalled. "How can you people *say* something like that? Are we not servants of light? Is it not our job to bring peace and love to this fallen world?"

Ethan calmly put his hand on my shoulder. "Milady...Sarai...as guardians, it's our sworn duty to guide our mortals back home to the Father. To help them make the choices that will optimize their spiritual and physical growth. Endangering their emotional welfare would only inhibit our mission."

"*Qué porquería*, are you listening to yourself?" I wrenched away from his hand, teeth grinding in righteous fury. "What good is emotional welfare if we're sheltering our mortals from doing what's right? You think standing against darkness and hatred is a matter of comfort? What if it was *your* kid over there sitting by themselves? Wouldn't you ache for someone to show them they aren't alone?"

"It's not that simple."

I slowly shook my head, his bold stature seemingly shrinking before my eyes. "What happened to all that chivalry you were spouting, Ethan? Aren't all the daughters of Heaven royalty?" I jabbed a thumb at Beth Starkovsky. "What about that one over there? Does she count or does the rule only apply when it's convenient?"

The other angels fell silent, stepping back as I approached my granddaughter. I understood the price of what I was about to ask of her. There was a good chance she wouldn't even yield to my voice, caving to the fearful paralysis of public opinion, but who would I be if I didn't at least try? I clenched my fists, opening my mouth to coax Dani across the cafeteria.

Then *he* entered the room.

A shadowy, hulking figure, taller than the double doors he came walking in through, his bare chest and back decorated with heavy scars. Broken chains dangled from his wrists, clinking against the armored plates sewn into his leather battle skirt. The nearest angel turned to look up at him, stumbling backward onto the floor in shock.

"Th-the...the *Demon of Wrath?*"

Those words reverberated off the walls and ceiling with an ungodly power, every last spirit freezing in place as though time itself had ground to a halt. The dark behemoth scanned the room, his blood-red eyes dancing from each table to the next. After what felt like an eternity, he roared at us in a deep, rumbling bass.

"Which one of these meat bags is Daniela Rivera?"

My stomach instantly dropped into my feet as an army of fingers pointed in our direction. This couldn't be happening.

This was Dani's replacement demon? One of the Seven Sins of Inferno? It wasn't fair. What did I—what did *she*—ever do to deserve this? As I stood there, petrified with denial, the Lord of Wrath came lumbering over.

Angels cowered out of his way, demons falling on their knees in adoration. Every step closer made me realize just how massive he really was, the top of my head barely reaching his chiseled six-pack abs. Somehow, I managed to push through my trepidation, willing myself between him and Dani as he rounded our table.

"Well now, ain't that adorable." The demon stopped only a couple yards away, peering down at me with a fanged grin. "You must be the competition, eh, short stack?"

I craned my neck upward, summoning all the confidence I could muster. "So, you're the infamous Lord of Wrath, huh? The stories made you sound a lot bigger."

My adversary leaned forward, stroking his bushy black beard in amusement. "They weren't talking about my *height*, sweetheart."

All the succubi in the room practically fainted on the spot, Jezazel looking particularly smitten. She crawled past me along the floor and proceeded to lick the demon's taloned feet. "Lord Belial...what an honor it is for you to grace us with your presence..."

"Hey, get off me," Belial growled. "Can't you see I'm trying to work?" He casually kicked Jezazel away, sending her skidding across the tiles. "I swear, you'd think I'm the Sin of Lust over here. Now then, let's take a gander at my newest target."

"You'll do nothing of the sort!" I snapped. "My granddaughter is a kind and devout follower of the light. You'll have no influence over her."

"We'll see about that..." Belial stretched forward a meaty claw, pushing me aside like a rag doll as he advanced on Daniela. She was busy gobbling up her empanadas, completely ignorant of the monster towering over her. He dropped down on one knee, nuzzling his face in her hair, his eyes rolling backward as he drew a deep breath through his nostrils. "Aaaaaaah, yessss...what a delicious aroma. The fear of judgment and loss...and something else..." He took another long whiff. "A touch of pride...how excellent. I can work with that."

"Get away from her!" I cried, picking myself up off the ground.

"Make me." Belial turned his gaze on Candace, rubbing his hands together. "Now for a game of 'stir the pot.' Where is this girl's demon?"

Diva stiffened up beside him, fighting back a swoon. "Here, my lord!"

"Mind if I take the reins for a bit?"

"You can take my reins any time you want," Diva giggled.

Belial knocked her down with a wink, moving to whisper in Candace's ear when her angel came storming out of the crowd. She was so quiet and mousy I hadn't even realized she was there, her scrawny little frame reminding me of a Chihuahua confronting a pit bull.

"Not so fast!" the angel said in a high, nasally voice. "Regardless of your rank, the Treaty of Heaven and Hell clearly states that no spirit is allowed to influence a human to which they aren't assigned. It's the celestial decree that governs balance and order on Earth. Even a cardinal demon isn't above the rules."

"Shut up, Abigail," Diva hissed. "Go take your hall monitor act someplace else. Or better yet, why don't you go back to hiding under the table like a good bottom feeder?"

"Abigail's right," I piped up. "If any diablo can tempt your human, then any angel can strengthen them as well. Is that what you want? Total chaos from both sides?"

"Everyone calm down," Belial grunted. "If you featherbacks want to cite the rules, then cite the rules. The Treaty's exact words are, 'No spirit shall influence a mortal outside of their domain.' But if you recall correctly, a spirit's domain is defined as both their human's household..."

"...And their immediate vicinity," I said, begrudgingly finishing the sentence.

Belial's smirk widened. "Exactly. And unless my eyes deceive me, these girls are sitting side by side. It doesn't get much more 'immediate' than that." He dismissed us with a wave of his hand, turning back to resume Candace's temptation. "Hey, I can tell you're the queen bee around here, aren't you?" he whispered. "Why you playin' second fiddle to Miss Taquitos over there? She's soaking up all the attention, stealing away all the cute boys. You need to put her in her place."

Candace looked at Dani, her expression darkening into a scowl. "Seriously though, you should probably go sit with that loser, Beth," she insisted. "You could give her some tips on how to dress for the 90's."

"Wait...*what?*" Dani wrinkled her forehead, anxiously clutching the lap of her blue jeans. "Why would you say that?"

"I just think the two of you have a lot in common," Candace replied. "Not everyone can pull off an elementary school outfit, but you do it way better than she does. You should totally give her some pointers. I bet she'd love hearing all about your fancy food experiments."

Dani stared at her last empanada, her voice quivering with embarrassment. "I just wanted to sit with you guys. We don't have to talk about my cooking if it bugs you."

"Don't be silly," Candace purred. "Nobody has a problem with your little Iron Chef spiel. This table simply isn't your scene."

"My scene?"

"Look around," Candace said, motioning to her fan club. "This isn't your average group of seniors, Dani. We're trendsetters. The future leaders of the world. It's a bit too high speed for someone that can't even name who they're wearing."

Dani scratched her head. "Who I'm *wearing?* Am I supposed to name my clothes?"

Candace and her crew promptly burst into laughter.

"Hey, leave her alone!" Hector yelled over them. "She's allowed to hang here as much as anyone else!"

"Th-that's right," Dani stammered, her face flushing a bright red. "I don't have to live by some ritzy dress code to be here. What matters is who we are inside."

The laughter grew even louder. "Oh, man, that's priceless," Candace said, wiping a tear from her eye. "You know what? Maybe your outfit isn't so bad after all. It just needs a bit more flavor." She turned to her tray of lasagna, scooping up a sizable chunk with her spork and flinging it at Dani's shirt. The orange glob splattered everywhere, speckling the remains of my granddaughter's lunch.

"What the—?" Dani leapt off the bench, watching in dismay as the pasta tumbled down her pants onto her shoes.

"C'mon, chef, don't let the food go to waste," Candace chuckled. "Five-second rule!"

Belial threw his head back, belting out a cackle of his own. "Sweet Lucifer, I love this kid!"

Dani grabbed a napkin, her eyes misting as she desperately tried to rub the lasagna from her clothes. How could I let this happen? In all the years I'd spent by her side, never had I witnessed such crippling humiliation. Such blatant cruelty. Was this the power of a cardinal demon? Or was it my fault? Did I let myself slip into complacency?

"Now for the coup de grâce," Belial said, setting his sights on Dani.

That was the final straw. I thrust out my hand, tapping into my connection with Heaven's light, projecting my soul's undying resolve into my open palm. It solidified in a burst of white flames, taking on the shape of a curved silvery blade.

I knew it was frowned upon for a spirit to strike down their counterpart. After all, it wasn't as though we could actually die. Not permanently at least, but we could still experience pain, and the time it would take for our bodily forms to reconstitute would afford a temporary reprieve. Even a few days alone with Daniela would give me the chance to hopefully undo the damage Belial had caused. It was a risky and ultimately futile strategy, inviting retaliation and disrupting the natural balance of things, but I no longer cared.

Tightening my grip on its golden hilt, I lunged forward, aiming to bury my sword in the demon's chest. Its gleaming tip was only inches away from lodging between his ribs when he caught it with his bare hand. The motion was almost too fast for me to see, the cutting edge of my blade resting helplessly against his dark gray skin.

Belial slowly turned to glare at me, the pupils of his crimson eyes narrowing into vertical slits. "You're a *feisty* one, aren't you?"

Before I could utter a word, he grabbed me by the wrist, hurling me over the lunch table into the middle of the cafeteria. I tumbled across the floor, sliding to a stop as he circled back to his prey.

"What's the matter, Dani?" Candace taunted, still sitting with her friends. "I thought you liked Italian food."

Belial knelt down beside Dani, his yellowed teeth flashing gleefully as he whispered in her ear. "That heartless wench is making you look like a fool in front of everyone. Are you just gonna stand there and take it? She hurt you, so hurt her back. It isn't revenge. It's justice."

Dani paused for a moment, the emotion draining from her face. Then came the wrath. It simmered just beneath the surface, cleverly disguised as a submissive grin.

"You know what? You're right," she said, returning to the table. "This wouldn't be so bad if I had something to wash down the lasagna."

Dani snatched up her carton of chocolate milk, popping open the tab while everyone watched in silence. She pretended to raise it to her lips, lurching forward at the last second to chuck it at Candace. The carton smacked her square in the jaw, milk splashing over her white tank top to reveal the stuffed push-up bra underneath.

"Suck on *that*, douchebag," Dani bellowed.

All eyes were on Candace now. She blinked hard at Dani, her stunned expression quickly melting into rage. "Gah! You dirty little skank!"

Candace scooped up another chunk of lasagna with her fingers and threw it as hard as she could, but this time Dani was ready. She ducked to the side, letting the pasta sail over her shoulder into a random boy's face.

He reached up to touch the slime, its lukewarm tomato sauce infecting him with equal fury. "Dude, what the *frick?*" The boy stood up and pitched a cup of yogurt back at Candace, narrowly missing, the glob of blueberry tart splattering one of her unsuspecting fangirls instead.

"FOOD FIGHT!" someone cried from the other side of the cafeteria.

"RIOT!" Belial added with a roar.

That's when all Hell broke loose.

The entire room full of students exploded into a frenzy, every drink and entree imaginable suddenly going airborne. Meanwhile, the demons had begun to channel their wicked powers, summoning the shadows from under each table and object to form weapons of pure, solidified darkness. They brandished pitchforks and daggers, lances and clubs, using the chaos as a perfect excuse to turn them on the surrounding angels.

I was still collecting myself on the ground when the nearest devil came at me with a studded mace. He brought it down with both hands, expecting the element of surprise to win him the kill, but he was far too slow.

I rolled sideways onto my feet, slicing his calf with my sword in a single fluid motion. He toppled forward onto his knees, crying out in agony as I slipped behind him. A flick of my wrist twirled the blade into a reverse grip, another driving it through the demon's back and out his chest. His face contorted painfully, his pale gray skin beginning to crack and flake off into embers. Then, with a muffled poof, he disintegrated into a pile of glowing ashes.

"Yield! Yield, foul beasts!"

A short distance away, I noticed Beth Starkovsky's angel struggling to defend her. She was crouched behind her lonely table, hiding from the edible crossfire of other students while he blindly swung his sword at a trio of demons. They continued to close in, weapons poised to skewer him at any moment.

Before I could think twice, my legs were racing to his aid, my arm winding up to unleash a wide horizontal sweep. The demons never even saw it coming, the edge of my blade severing all three of their heads without any resistance. Their bodies crumbled into cinders, vanishing from the mortal realm as Beth's angel looked up at me.

"Many thanks," he said, gasping for breath.

"What's your name, amigo?"

"Malachi."

"Get your human out of here, Malachi. I'll cover you."

The angel nodded, vaulting over the table to Beth's side. Her small imp of a demon was still perched on her shoulder, hissing at me like a disgruntled cat. Malachi simply grabbed him by the tail, flinging him into the crowd of brawling spirits, then leaned over to whisper in Beth's ear. She promptly responded by snatching a food tray off the table, using it for a shield as she made a break for the exit. Malachi followed closely behind, watching for any incoming attacks while I cleared the path ahead.

The cafeteria had turned into a bloodbath, adults scrambling to regain control as kids darted back and forth, caked from head to toe in a patchwork of filth. The walls and ceiling shared a similar coat of paint, puddles of Gatorade and soda creating an oil slick all over the floor. As for the spiritual battle, combatants of both sides were dropping left and right, vanquished demons bursting to ash while their angelic rivals dissolved into clouds of golden dust.

I weaved through the fray, leaping over fallen comrades, embers pelting me in the face with every flash of my blade. After leaving behind a wake of destruction, Beth and Malachi managed to reach the double doors, escaping to safety as I went to search for Daniela. She was halfway across the room, emptying her bowl of rice and beans down the back of Candace's shirt.

Belial stood over them, laughing at the top of his lungs, fluttering his hands through the air as though manipulating the strings of a marionette. "Dance, my puppets! Dance!"

I clenched my jaw, taking a step forward to challenge him when I noticed Jezazel standing between us. Her one visible eye peered at me through her curtain of greasy hair, a malicious grin twisting her mouth into a crescent.

"Where do you think *you're* going?" she croaked. "We've got a score to settle, Judge Prudy."

Jezazel raised her hands in front of her, summoning the nearby shadows. They snaked up from the ground like pitch-black tentacles, coalescing over her gnarled fingernails. Each steadily grew longer and sharper, hardening to become a foot-long dagger unto itself.

I answered with a silent threat of my own, materializing a second sword into my free hand with a flash of holy fire. It was identical to the first—a curved scimitar made of celestial steel—the length of its blade gleaming hungrily at my opponent.

For a few nerve-racking seconds, we simply stared at each other, locked in a heated game of mental chicken. Who would be the first to move? Would it be a rush, a feint or a cowardly retreat? It was impossible for me to read the truth in her cold, lifeless eye, but there was one thing I could tell we had in common.

We both intended to end this quickly.

Then I saw it. The shifting of her weight. Muscles tensing in her right bicep. It didn't surprise me that she would go for my neck, but the speed of her charge was unlike any of the other demons, closing the distance in a heartbeat. I deflected the initial thrust, her bladed nails grazing my shoulder as I swung my other sword. It tore through the air, about to cleave her skull in two when she blocked it with her opposing claw. Sparks erupted from the point of contact, steel grinding against hardened shadow.

"Not bad," Jezazel said, grabbing hold of my blades. "I guess there's a bit more to you than just a pretty face."

"You don't know the half of it."

I whipped myself forward, headbutting her in the nose. The blow sent a ripple of pain down my spine, but it was well worth the sacrifice. Jezazel staggered backwards, screeching in anguish, leaving herself wide open as she released my swords. I lunged, my thoughts already moving on to Dani and how I was going to rescue her.

Kuh-PSSSH!

The next thing I knew, I was lying sideways on the ground. Something had lashed me across my left forearm, specks of golden dust bleeding from the wound. I looked up to find Diva sauntering over, smugly tossing her fiery blue hair.

She held a long whip in her hand, its shadowy coils barbed with fragments of shattered bone. "Mind if I cut in?"

Jezazel swiftly recovered from my impromptu head bash, giving Diva an appreciative nod. "It's about time you showed up. Ready to tag team this featherback?"

The two demons began to advance, both grinning menacingly as they raised their weapons. I desperately tried to shimmy away on my elbows, willing my body to get up, but the searing pain in my arm sapped me of any strength. I couldn't do it. I couldn't let them win. Not when Daniela was counting on me. Not if it meant leaving her alone with the Demon of Wrath.

I grit my teeth, screaming defiantly at my assailants.

They charged.

Then came the freight train. Or rather, a heavy metal shield, long and rectangular. It smashed into both demons from the side, launching them across the floor through a row of tables.

"*Ethan?*"

The angel lowered his shield, reaching down to help lift me up. "Are you hurt, Milady?"

"Just a scratch." I raised a blade to my lips, biting down on the flat so that my spare hand could accept his.

"Please forgive my delay," Ethan said, gently hoisting me onto my feet. "I had quite a few bandits to slaughter."

"I know the feeling." I clutched my swords, struggling to ignore the throb in my left arm as we watched the two succubi pick themselves back up. "So, what's the plan? I take Diva, you take Jezazel?"

Ethan shook his head. "Save your strength. Leave them both to me."

I stared at him, furrowing my brow. "W-what? I don't need you to fight for me. If this is your idea of honor—"

"This isn't about chivalry," Ethan said flatly. "You're the one that has to get to Dani. You have to stop Belial and end this madness."

"You expect me to run away and leave you outnumbered? Those two aren't your standard diablitos."

Ethan turned to the approaching threat, crouching into a fighting stance. "A simple 'thank you' would suffice."

"All you have is a shield!"

"I have a lot more than that..." Ethan closed his eyes and took a deep breath, his body quickly igniting in a shroud of white flames. They condensed over his pants and tunic, arms and head, crystallizing into a full suit of shimmering armor. The last of his holy fire leapt into his open hand, fading away to reveal a gilded broadsword—the true emblem of a heavenly knight. He gave it a masterful flourish, clanging it against his pavise shield for maximum intimidation.

"Show-off."

Ethan barreled forward, letting out a savage roar. The sight of his dragon-crested shield sent the succubi into full retreat. The other surrounding demons began to flee as well, leaving me with a clear path to Dani and Belial. I broke into a sprint, my hopes and fears waiting for me side by side when a voice thundered over the chaos, so loud even my divine eardrums were ringing.

"DANIELA RIVERA!"

All at once, the whole cafeteria fell silent and still. Every angel, demon and child turned to find Mr. Elliot standing at the main entrance with a bullhorn in his hand. His face was red with anger, veins popping from his temples.

"PRINCIPAL'S OFFICE! NOW!"

Chapter 3

JUDGE AND JURY

HOW DID IT COME TO THIS? One minute, we're chomping down mama's empanadas. The next, we're sitting on death row. At least that's what it felt like. It was always my mission to do everything by the book. To fight for nothing less than perfection in everything Dani said or did, but inciting anarchy in the halls of learning?

Who *was* this person?

I'm not sure I knew anymore. I could already see her once promising life swirling down the toilet bowl. She'd likely drop out of school before long, forsaking her dreams of becoming a chef to pursue a criminal career in gourmet violence. Robbing people at toast point, or maybe even a drive-by fruiting. Eventually, she'd hit the wrong person with a peanut allergy and that would be it. Convicted murderer walking the gallows for real. The thought sent a shiver running through my body.

As for Dani herself, she seemed to be taking things a lot better than I was. She crossed one leg over the other, glancing around the principal's waiting room with a look of sheer boredom. We were the only ones present, Belial's massive rump taking up two seats on the other side of her.

That miserable *puerco*. He sat there happy as a clam, patting an unfamiliar rhythm on his knees. "Sweet Lucifer, that was a blast," he muttered. "I wonder how many of you featherbacks got dusted back at the cafeteria. You guys really got saved by the bell. Or should I say, 'bullhorn.'"

"*Cállate, Gordo!*" I snapped.

"Kaiya-*whatnow?* Are you one of those Chinese angels?"

"I said, 'Shut your mouth, Gordo.'"

"What the heaven is a Gordo?"

"You are."

Belial rubbed his shiny bald head. "Huh. I'll take that as a compliment."

I tightly folded my arms, fuming at his apathy. "What's the illustrious Demon of Wrath doing with a regular girl like Dani in the first place? Don't you have bigger fish to fry?"

"What's the matter, short stack? Already missing that pushover, Gigglewarts?"

"My name is Sarai," I growled. "And is that what this is about? Inferno sent you to punish me for besting one of your minions?"

Belial leaned around Dani, peering at me with a condescending glint in his eyes. "Do you honestly think this is about you? Don't be so vain. The boss and I couldn't care less who you are. All you need to know is that Satan works in mysterious ways."

"I should report you to the arch-seraphs," I said, grinding my teeth.

"For what, pray tell?"

"For disrupting the balance of light and darkness. For violating the sanctity of free will. Because of you and that riot, dozens of kids will be subjected to temptation without their angel to offer support."

Belial slouched back in his chairs, smirking up at the ceiling. "You seriously wanna nark me? Go right ahead. Tell Arch-seraph Remiel and his enforcers all about how it started. How I was minding my own business, following the Treaty of Heaven and Hell to the letter when my angelic counterpart decided to have a pissy fit because I was gaining some traction. If I recall correctly, *yours* was the first sword to be swung, was it not?"

My jaw went slack, eyes bulging as the realization finally sank in. It was me. *I* was the first one to show aggression, giving him the license he needed to escalate. To think Candace's angel and I had the gall to lecture him about the rules when he knew them far better than we did. He understood every last pretense and loophole, using the situation as bait to destroy my credibility.

"It really is a shame," Belial said in mock lamentation. "My people were just trying to do their civic duty, guiding souls to Inferno, but you and your pack of bloodthirsty savages simply couldn't take it. Because of you, dozens of kids will be forced to play Charades and wear high-water pants without their demon to convince them otherwise."

"You're such a despicable sack of pus."

"Thanks. If you'd pull that flag pole out of your butt, you wouldn't be so bad either...for a featherback."

That term. *Featherback.* Every time I heard it, I wanted to punch my fist through a wall. Granted, as a spirit, I could already do that with incredible ease, but still, there was something about that word I just couldn't shake. Contrary to the medieval stereotype, we angels didn't even have any wings. It was like he was calling our entire existence a lie, as though we were nothing more than fictional poultry. I wanted to fire back with something witty, brainstorming a few equally ironic insults. Perhaps "hornhead," or maybe "goatface."

No. Those would only make him laugh. Besides, there was always the occasional demon that actually fit those descriptions. I stared down at the carpet, straining for something better when the door to the principal's office creaked open.

A boy with frizzy blond hair and baggy cargo shorts came sauntering out. He seemed about Dani's age, flanked by his two designated spirits. The angel trudged along with a defeated gait, head down, shoulders slumped, his face obscured behind a veil of long golden hair. His demon was the exact opposite. A snarky-looking man with yellow eyes and a black goatee, beaming as if he'd just won the Super Bowl.

Belial jumped to his feet as soon as he saw him, his face lighting up. "Yuriel? Dude, is that you?"

The demon regarded him with matching excitement. "Belial! How's it goin', buddy? You find yourself a new human?"

"Yup. That piece of trash right over there," Belial said, bobbing his head at Daniela. "We just got bagged for throwing a huge food fight in the cafeteria. It was pretty epic."

"Son of a banshee, I wish I could've been there."

"Right? What a crazy coincidence that we ended up at the same school."

The demon scratched his head, grinning sheepishly. "Weeeeell, about that...I kinda already got my human expelled."

Belial gaped in amazement. "On the first day of school? You gotta be kiddin' me! What for?"

"Security caught him with a gallon bag of weed."

"Holy smokes!"

"Literally."

A woman's voice called from inside the principal's office, interrupting the celebration. "Mr. Meechum, we aren't done here!"

The boy with the frizzy hair glanced over his shoulder, a sharpened edge in his tone. "I don't need any more of your blabbing, Kingsley. If you guys are gonna book me, then let's get it over with." A police officer emerged from the office and took the boy by his arm, ushering him into the hallway. "Later, losers! I never liked this place anyway!"

"Guess I'll have to catch up with you later," the boy's demon said, waving goodbye to Belial. "'Til we meet again..." He ducked into the hall after his human, disappearing around the corner as the mopey angel gave chase.

Once they were safely out of earshot, Belial grumbled to himself, his expression darkening. "The nerve of that over-achieving little snot. How could he get himself kicked out when I only just got here?"

"Daniela Rivera."

The three of us looked to the doorway of Principal Kingsley's office, spotting the headmaster herself leaning against the frame. She wore a navy-blue pantsuit and a pair of thick-rimmed glasses, her grizzled gray hair neatly tied back in a bun. I'd seen her several times over the last few years, mostly from afar. Assemblies and sporting events. She always seemed so pleasant and approachable, but not today. There was a scathing weariness behind those pale blue eyes. A sympathy that was long past its expiration date.

"Well? What are you waiting for?" she said, clapping her hands. "Inside, young lady."

Dani picked up her backpack and traipsed across the reception area, slipping past Kingsley into the office. Belial and I closely followed, panic washing over me as the soundproof door clicked shut behind us. Even in life, I'd never had the misfortune of being reprimanded by a principal. What kind of gruesome tortures were in store for us? Would anyone hear the twisted agony of Dani's screams?

The room appeared harmless enough. No guillotines or iron maidens. Only a padded chair in the center. It faced a wooden desk with a computer on top, some framed credentials hanging on the wall above it. In the far corner stood an angel, presumably Kingsley's. She was tall and muscular with a braided rope of hair draping over her shoulder. Instead of the usual white robes, she had a leather dress covered with various furs, plates of steel fastened over her chest, arms and forehead.

Was she some kind of soldier? Was *I* the one about to be tortured?

"Who in perdition are *you* supposed to be?" Belial said, motioning to the angel.

"I am Brynhildr," she replied flatly. "Daughter of Ragnar and Thorganna. Heir of line Erikson and former sage of the Nords."

"Oh yeah? Well, I'm the Queen of England."

Brynhildr glared at him without a twitch of amusement. "Jest at your own peril. Know also that I am a hunter-class angel, specially trained to subdue unruly spirits. Even a demon of your renown would not leave this place unharmed should you offend its sovereignty."

Belial sarcastically threw his hands in the air. "Oooooh, scary."

"Care to test me?" She lifted her arm, materializing a rune-etched battle axe into her grip.

"Nope, nope, let's all be cool here," I insisted. "Everybody's tranquilo...right, Gordo?"

"Whatever," he said, pursing his lips. "I'll wait and see how this plays out."

"Please sit," Kingsley said, circling around to her desk. Dani obliged, walking past Belial and me to grab the padded chair. "Now then, Mr. Elliot tells me you were the one who instigated that fiasco in the cafeteria. Would you mind explaining yourself?"

"I wasn't the one who started it," Dani grunted. "It was Candace McNairy."

"Mr. Elliot says he saw you throw a carton of milk at her."

"Apparently, he missed the part where she slathered me with lasagna."

Kingsley drummed her fingers on the desk. "Miss McNairy has always been a model student. She's never had a history of violent or malicious behavior."

"Neither have I," Dani shot back. "Look at me." She pulled down the bottom of her shirt, gesturing to the stains running from her collar all the way to her shoes. "You think I did this to myself?"

Kingsley shifted uncomfortably. "And what exactly provoked this...altercation?"

"Honestly, I'm not really sure," Dani replied. "Candace and I seemed to get along okay at first. I mentioned that I wanted to be a chef after going to college and then she just...blew up at me. She started making fun of my clothes, telling me I should sit somewhere else. You could ask Hector Torres. He saw the whole thing."

"What would possess her to do something like that?" Kingsley mused.

"Gee, I have no idea," Belial chuckled.

"Why don't you pull her in here and ask her?" Dani suggested.

Kingsley rested her elbows on the desk, steepling her fingers. "I don't think you fully understand the gravity of the situation," she said, slightly lowering her voice. "Candace's father is a very reputable prosecuting attorney. He has quite a record of pushing lawsuits and trumping up charges against people who cross his family. I would hate to see a promising girl like you fall into his crosshairs."

Dani and I stiffened at her subtle threat, both our minds racing to guess the implications.

"Man, that Candace brat is the gift that keeps on giving," Belial chimed in.

"W-what are you saying?" Dani stammered. "Am I going to get arrested?"

Kingsley shook her head. "Of course not. Even if smearing food on someone were a federal crime, Mr. Elliot had a clear view of Candace throwing lasagna at an innocent bystander. Her dad wouldn't be able to press any kind of charges without implicating his own daughter as well."

Dani relaxed her shoulders. "So...does this mean I'm off the hook?"

"Legally? Yes. But you still helped initiate the food fight and left our cafeteria in ruins. Somebody has to take responsibility."

"Here it comes," Belial said, rubbing his hands together. "The sentencing..."

I clenched my fists, bracing for Dani's imminent punishment. What would it be, I wondered. Detention? Suspension? Tickle torture? Then a raspy voice came out of nowhere, seemingly echoing my next thought.

"Burn 'em in oil!"

I recoiled in surprise, frantically scanning the room for a source. A pair of misshapen eyes peeked up from behind Kingsley's desk, one small and watery, the other huge and bulbous. They flicked wildly between me and Belial, searching our faces for what I assumed was approval.

"Please forgive Mistress Kingsley's demon," Brynhildr said, clutching her axe. "Skunkwad is a more simple-minded breed of evil, and deciding a student's penance is his favorite game."

"Heh, heh...burn 'em in oil."

"*Skunkwad?*" I said, craning my neck. "*That's* his name?"

"Yeah, yeah! Lots of fire!" A shriveled hunchback emerged from behind the desk, grinning happily with a mouthful of rotten teeth. If I'd had a mortal stomach, I would've vomited at the sight of him.

"Aaaaw, he's adorable," Belial said, relishing my disgust.

Kingsley sat back in her chair, studying Daniela. "Now then...what to do with you. This one incident has managed to earn you quite the rap sheet. Littering. Disorderly conduct. Violence against another student. Destruction of property, both public and private."

"Heh, heh, yeah, baby!" Skunkwad cheered. "Burn 'em in oil!"

I lashed a finger at the demon, snapping under the pressure. "Would you *please* knock it off with the stupid oil thing?"

He cowered back behind the desk, his voice trembling. "B-b-burn 'em in...jello?"

"As you can imagine, these infractions are very serious," Kingsley continued. "Someone could've been injured, and my phone is going to melt once all the parents get word of this." She let out a deep sigh. "It's absolutely ridiculous. The first day of school and we've already got World War III competing with an expulsion."

"Heh, heh, burn 'em at the stake!"

"Hey, at least he's mixing it up now," Belial added.

"Yeah, yeah! Bonfire! Big bonfire! All the bodies!"

"No one is going to burn this girl at the stake," Brynhildr scolded. "When I was a lass, we Viking folk would correct the youth with a tender beating. Five clubs to the shin would suffice. Broken bones build character."

"Oh, this is gettin' *good*," Belial chuckled.

"You're not helping!" I cried at both of them.

"Heh, heh...ffffire..."

Kingsley glanced up at the ceiling, her eyes going out of focus as if actually considering all of the psychobabble. After a tense moment of reflection, she leaned forward again, clasping her hands. "Well, Dani, this kind of thing would normally warrant a suspension, but since this is your first offense ever, and you certainly weren't the only culprit involved, I'm willing to give you some slack."

"A warning?" Dani asked, perking up.

"Detention. You'll be staying after school to help the janitors clean the mess you made in the cafeteria."

Dani's jaw dropped. "*What? Me?* What about everyone else? What about Candace?"

"She'll be joining you as well. A little bit of teamwork might do the two of you some good."

"But it could take *hours* to clean the cafeteria! There was stuff on the ceiling!"

"You should've thought of that before playing with your food."

"That's bullcrap!" Dani groaned. "This is so unfair!"

"Yeah, you tell her," Belial said, placing a hand on Dani's shoulder.

Kingsley narrowed her eyes. "You want to talk about fairness? How about the poor janitors that'll have to mop up alongside you? How about all the kids that wanted to eat in peace before getting caught up in your mayhem? Actions have consequences, young lady. You're lucky I'm not issuing a second expulsion today."

"Heaven forbid," Dani said, smoldering with contempt. "Wouldn't want any rumors floating around the district about a school with behavioral problems, would we?" She stood up, clutching the strap of her backpack. "Are we done here?"

"I guess we are," Kingsley shrugged, "but you're skating on some pretty thin ice, Miss Rivera, both with me *and* the McNairys. One more stunt like today's and your head will be underwater. I'll be calling your parents to let them know the situation you're in."

"Thanks a million." With that, Dani pivoted on her heels and stormed over to the door, angrily flinging it open. As her footsteps faded into the hall, Belial's lips curled into a fiendish grin.

"Oh, we're far from done, little girl," he whispered loud enough for me to hear. "If a small-time demon can get a kid expelled, so can I…"

Chapter 4
Sanctuary Lost

THE DRIVE BACK HOME was a lot longer than I expected. Dani sat up front in her usual spot, brooding with her arms folded. Carmen was dying to break the awkward silence, sneaking her daughter an occasional sideways glance, but the words never came.

Where would she even start? It was natural for a parent to sympathize with their child. She knew Dani would never have acted up without good reason, yet that didn't change the fact that she had. It probably made Carmen question whether or not the fault was somehow her own. Was it something she said or did? A bad example? Maybe Dani had gotten the idea from somewhere online. The mystery of it all was eating away at her, and she wasn't the only one.

"Sounds like you guys had a wild day," Laila said, reeling on the van's middle bench beside me. "I never thought Dani was capable of all that. It's beyond loco."

I slouched back against the seat, letting out an exasperated sigh. "Tell me about it. Things were going fine until Gordo showed up."

I could sense Belial smirking in the row behind us, quietly eavesdropping. It would've been nice to vent my frustrations in confidence, but that was part and parcel of having a demonic counterpart. Privacy came at a premium. Fortunately, Laila had picked up on my report about the principal's office, reminding me of a skill the big monster didn't possess.

"*So, can we talk about the elephant in the room here?*" she said in fluent Spanish. "*Is he really the Lord of Wrath?*"

I flashed a faint smile, replying in the same dialect. "*I'm afraid so. His influence is much stronger than any demon I've crossed before. He was able to spark a fight between Dani and that blonde egomaniac in a matter of seconds. I tried to get through to her, but it was no use. Dani wouldn't listen.*"

"Hey, enough with the gibberish," Belial grunted. "What are you featherbacks yammering on about?"

"Maybe if you clean out that ear wax and pay attention, you'll learn something," Laila hissed over the back of her seat.

I had to hand it to her. She always had a way of putting things delicately. The best part was that she wasn't even being sarcastic. For us angels, language was never an obstacle. Without the limitations of a mortal brain, we could technically speak and understand any tongue we wanted. A perk of our connection to the light, I guess you could say.

Demons, however, were a totally different animal. They weren't bound to any region or culture, aimlessly roaming the earth since the dawn of time. Learning the ways of men—how they speak, how they think, how they *hunger*—has only ever been for a singular purpose: humanity's spiritual destruction. And the only method? Observation, pure and simple.

Still, with billions of mortals to choose from, thousands of years to study and hone their craft, I could scarcely imagine how much knowledge a demon could obtain. My old nemesis, Gigglewarts, was fluent in over sixteen different languages and customs, including Russian, German, Arabic, Hebrew and Spanish. I didn't expect Belial to give me an honest answer as to which ones he'd assimilated, but if my native tongue was missing from the list, I was willing to press my advantage.

"*How's my son?*" I asked Laila. "*Does he already know what happened?*"

She glanced down at the floor. "*The principal called earlier today and gave him the whole story. He was pretty worried at first, but you know Tulio. He snapped right back. Cracked a joke or two in front of Carmen to take the edge off.*"

"*That's my boy. And Scarvin?*"

"*Behaving himself fairly well. He got Tulio to binge-watch a couple hours of* Family Guy *but that's about it.*"

"*I wonder how he's going to react to our new house guest,*" I said, peering over my shoulder.

"*I suppose we're about to find out.*"

The van lurched to the side, pulling into the Rivera Family driveway. Thanks to Principal Kingsley's detention, we'd arrived several hours later than normal, the sun already dipping below the San Gabriel Mountains. Stars peppered the indigo sky, timidly casting their brilliance as the streetlamps awakened to drown them out. The rest of the neighborhood was quiet and peaceful, light peeking through the windows of each identically built ranch-style house.

"Home sweet home," Carmen said, trying to lighten the mood.

Dani rolled her eyes and popped open the passenger side door, eagerly making her escape onto the concrete. We both knew there was nothing "sweet" about an impending lecture. She'd already explained herself a thousand times to every teacher, student and janitor that crossed her path. At this point, I could understand why she'd just want to leave the day behind. Maybe if she could somehow forget, her parents would too.

The rest of us scrambled out of the van in pursuit, following Dani up the paved walkway to the front door. She twisted the knob, finding it locked, but instead of breaking out her key, she immediately started hammering the ringer button. The porch light flickered on in reply, and the door slowly creaked open to reveal a stout middle-aged man. He was about a foot taller than Dani with pudgy cheeks and thinning black hair. Oxygen tubes draped over his ears and under his nose, partially obscuring his shaggy mustache.

"Hey there, Mija," he said, putting on a smile. "Welcome back."

Dani stared at the ground, refusing to meet his gaze. "Hey, Dad."

"You girls got here right on time. Dinner's almost ready."

"Thanks, but I'm not hungry," Dani said, slipping past him.

Carmen approached the doorway, giving the man's arm a reassuring squeeze. "Don't worry, Tulio. I'm sure she just needs a little coaxing."

"Yeah, like a cattle prod to the rear," Belial said, barging through the humans into the house. He placed his hands on his hips, glaring around at the humble decor. It was your typical twenty-first century living room—a couple of plush couches and a coffee table arranged in front of a flat screen TV. The walls were decorated with fanciful paintings and a large crucifix, an array of family portraits standing pristinely over the fireplace mantel. "Sweet Lucifer, what kind of musty old convent are we livin' in here? Where's all the booze and cocaine? These people better at least have HBO."

The sound of his voice drew a pair of spirits from the kitchen. The first was Tulio's angel, Kemuel, a bulky colossus with a mohawk and painted tribal markings covering his weathered bronze skin. He froze the moment he spotted Belial, his eyes widening at me and Laila in horrified confusion.

Strolling in behind him was a gangly, implike demon with a hook nose and a single broken horn protruding from his forehead. He gave a similar reaction, but rather than gawk speechlessly, he took a step forward, dropping onto one knee with a bow.

"L-L-Lord Belial! What an unexpected honor," the demon said, his voice slightly quivering. "Had I known you'd be replacing Gigglewarts, I would've—"

"Yeah, that's great, keep it in your pants, Tiny Tim," Belial shrugged without even bothering to glance at him.

"Scarvin," the demon replied.

"Excuse you?"

"Scarvin. It's my name, Sir. If we're going to be sharing a household, it might behoove us to get acquainted."

"I think we just did," Belial said, turning back to Daniela. "Glad *that's* over."

Carmen closed the front door behind her, leaning down to help Tulio with his personal oxygen tank. Its carrier looked like a small suitcase on wheels, the metal canister inside clinking around as she pulled on the handle. Tulio made sure to match her stride so that the rubber tubes extending from it didn't go taut around his head, carefully hobbling into the living room to confront his daughter. Dani had thrown herself onto the nearest couch, her face buried in one of the cushions.

"Are you sure I couldn't interest you in a bowl of risotto?" Tulio asked, patting her on the back. "I added extra parmesan just the way you like it."

"My life is over," Dani said, her groan muffled by the cushion.

"Well, that sucks," Tulio replied, grinning playfully. "I guess it means we'll have to turn your room into that art studio Mom always wanted."

Dani rolled over with a pout. "Don't even think about it."

"What's the big deal? If your life's over, who cares if we donate your stuff to the nearest homeless shelter? I'm sure those guys would *love* your sparkly vampire bedspread."

"You know what I mean," Dani grunted. "The entire school is talking trash about me. Half of them think I'm some kind of violent psychopath with anger management issues. The rest are saying I'm a two-faced bully."

Tulio perched himself on the arm of the couch, tilting his head sympathetically. "Mija, you should've told me you were gonna throw your lunch at a cheerleader. I would've packed you a fat bean burrito with some ghost peppers in it."

"She wasn't a cheerleader, Dad. She's from the debate team."

"Two burritos then?"

"She's one of the most popular kids in school."

"Extra greasy?"

"This isn't a joke!" Dani bellowed. "Candace made me a laughing stock! My clothes are wrecked and I just spent three hours scrubbing peanut butter off the cafeteria walls! How am I ever going to live this down?"

The room fell deathly quiet, the raspy inhalations of Tulio's oxygen tank the only sound. His expression sobered, his tone finally becoming serious. "Dani...do you want to tell us what really happened?"

She sat up on the seat of the couch, hugging her legs. "I just wanted to make friends," Dani whispered. "They invited me to eat with them so I thought we were cool. But then they...they started *attacking* me. They said I didn't belong there anymore." Her eyes began to well with tears. "Maybe they're right."

"Mija..." Carmen rounded the coffee table, sliding onto the couch beside her. "Not everyone deserves your friendship, Dani. Some people see the good in us and want to be a part of it. Others...feel threatened. Jealous. They want to tear down what they don't have or can't understand. If they'd rather not have you around, then you're all the better for it."

"They didn't have the right to make fun of me. To ruin my clothes."

"This wasn't the first time people have mistreated you," Tulio cut in. "Usually, you're so great at walking away and rolling with the punches. What made you lash out at them?"

Dani pressed her chin to her knees. "I...I don't know...I was just so angry. They needed to pay for what they did."

"Yes, that's right," Belial said, levitating into the air. He drifted upside down over the couch, bringing his lips to her ear. "Those arrogant whelps deserved what they got. They needed to feel your pain. Your hatred."

"Don't listen to him!" I shouted at Dani. "He's trying to stoke your emotions!"

"I know it's hard to turn the other cheek when people do us wrong," Carmen said, "but it's so important that we never sink to their level. We have to be better than that."

"Why should we always have to be the victim?" Dani snapped. "If we don't put bullies in their place, they'll keep on terrorizing the innocent."

"That's what the authorities are for," Tulio added. "If someone breaks the rules or picks on you, they need to be reported so that justice can be dealt fairly."

Dani sprang from the couch, absolutely livid. "Justice? Everybody saw what Candace did to me, yet *I'm* the one being branded as a bully! Even if I'd wanted to report her, Principal Kingsley is scared stiff of Candace's dad. How can we trust the system when the whole thing is rigged?"

"YES," Belial roared. "Everything's corrupt! Everything's broken! Burn it all to the ground!"

"Stop it!" I cried, rushing to Dani's side. "Escúchame, mi amor, this isn't you. The girl I know is loving and kind. Don't let vengeance consume you."

Tulio slowly raised his hands, desperately trying to calm his daughter. "Listen, Mija, I get it. The world isn't nearly as fair as it should be, but there has to be a line we don't cross. If we choose to—"

"You expect me to roll over for that spoiled, selfish cow?" Dani demanded. "Screw her! Screw everyone!" She turned away and stalked to the end of the hall, slamming her door as she disappeared into her bedroom.

"Daniela Isabel Rivera, you get your butt back here right now!" Carmen yelled after her.

"You heard the lady!" I chimed in as well. "Since when do you treat your parents like that?"

No response came.

Tulio lifted himself off the couch with a sigh, grabbing his oxygen tank as he headed into the darkened hallway. The journey was only a dozen feet or so, but it was enough to leave him wheezing by the time he reached the bedroom door. He knocked softly and waited, pressing his ear to the wood after a few moments of silence.

"Mija...I know how frustrated you are...but you can't take it out on everyone else," he panted. "You owe your mom and I...an apology."

"Just leave me alone," Dani hissed from inside.

"You'll feel a lot better with a full stomach," Tulio replied. "Come on out and have some risotto. We can relax and talk through this."

"There's nothing left to talk about."

"Then you shouldn't have a problem coming out for dinner."

"What do *you* care?"

Tulio furrowed his brow. "I'm your father. Of course I care about you."

"Really? Is that why you spent my entire childhood working nonstop at the shipyard? Is it the reason you got yourself sick and forced Mom to keep us afloat?"

"*Mija!*" Carmen stomped into the hallway, eyes wide in shock, opening her mouth to protest, but Tulio stopped her with a shake of his head.

"I...I'm sorry," he said, choking on the words. "You needed me all those years, but I didn't see it. I didn't realize what I was missing until God clocked me out...but I'm here now. I love you. I've always loved you. Let me make the most of what we have left."

"It's too late to make up for lost time," Dani answered.

Her dad's voice broke into a sob, tears streaming down his face. "Let me try, Mija. Please. There's no telling how many more dinner tables we'll get to share together. Don't waste them hating me alone in your room."

Dani paused for a second, measuring his truth against her bitterness, then delivered the final blow. "Go away. I don't need you. I never did."

Tulio rested his forehead against the door, sorrow dripping from his nose and chin. I could tell how badly he wanted to take her in his arms, to hold her tight like he did when she was little and never let go, but there was no crossing the rift between them. Not anymore. He staggered back down the hall, shoulders slumped in defeat, Carmen reaching out to offer a consoling embrace.

Meanwhile, Belial had returned to the living room floor, his yellowed fangs exposed in a triumphant grin. "Bravo!" he said with a slow clap. "Excellent performances all around. I gotta say, that girl is an absolute *firecracker*. I barely had to give her a push and she went nuclear."

"*Come on, Sweetheart. Let's try that dinner of yours*," Carmen whispered in Spanish.

Tulio nodded, leaning on her as they crept their way into the kitchen.

The other spirits and I exchanged glances, silently deciding how to interpret what had just transpired. Laila took a step towards me, muttering in the same linguistic code as our mortals. "*You should go check on Dani. The rest of us will try to keep the big guy distracted.*"

"Hey! I told you featherbacks to knock that off," Belial growled. "I swear, is there a fricking soul in this house that *doesn't* speak elvish?" He turned to the demon beside him, anxiously tapping his foot. "What about you, Starvin?"

"*Scarvin*," the imp corrected.

"Yeah, whatever, you understand any of this garbage?"

Scarvin's eyes darted between Laila and me, the faintest trace of a smile playing on his lips. Had Belial cared enough to actually get acquainted, he would've discovered that we and our resident demon shared a very unique relationship. Like any tempter, Scarvin's job was to inspire sin, fear, doubt and selfishness, feeding off the darkness of those tenets.

The problem was Dani's parents. As devout believers of the Father, their household was a veritable wasteland for evil, especially after Tulio became diagnosed with COPD. Hence, a bargain was struck. We angels would allow Scarvin to entertain himself as long as his mischief never threatened the spiritual welfare of our mortals. A controlled burn, so to speak, as opposed to the raging wildfire that was Belial.

Over the years, Scarvin had gleaned quite a bit from us and the Riveras. Spanish, cooperation, and a trait that could almost be described as loyalty. He enjoyed this domain and our tentative alliance. At a minimum, he knew we would treat him much better than his new coworker. As Belial waited for an answer to his question, Scarvin quickly whipped up something we angels couldn't—a lie.

"Forgive me, my lord, but I can't make heads or tails of it. I'm afraid their breed of gobbledygook has a fairly steep learning curve."

"Son of a banshee," Belial grunted. "Those stupid featherbacks are really gonna make me work for this."

"Come now, my lord, don't let the peons vex you. We need only to kill your boredom." Scarvin snapped his fingers, his expression brightening as if he'd suddenly remembered something. "Do you fancy playing with cards, my lord? Gambling, perhaps?"

Belial stroked his beard, frowning in consideration. "I do love a good wager. You know how to play poker?"

"Of course, my lord. What manner of hellspawn would I be if I didn't? If memory serves, there should be an old deck of cards up in the attic. Would you care to join me?"

Belial peered into the kitchen, studying the humans as they quietly chatted over their bowls of risotto. After a moment of hesitation, he finally surrendered to his own pleasures, nodding at his cohort with approval. "You know what, Starkin? You've got yourself a game. Lead the way."

The imp tossed me a coy smirk, then drifted into the air, beckoning to the Sin of Wrath as he vanished into the ceiling. The rest of us watched Belial float after him, waiting until he was fully out of sight before relaxing into a chuckle.

"Looks like we owe Scarvin another few hours of *Family Guy*," I said, nudging Laila with my elbow.

"Sounds fair to me," she replied. "Go take care of Dani. Kemuel and I will see what we can salvage from the others."

I bobbed my head in agreement, hurrying into the hallway to pass through Dani's bedroom door. The moment I cleared the alder wood, her whimpers filled my ears. She was curled up at the edge of her bed, arms wrapped around her pillow, using it to dry her tears. Surrounded by her knick-knacks and wall-mounted movie posters, this place was supposed to be her sanctuary. The one piece of square footage in the world where she could leave her troubles behind. Where she could feel safe and loved. Now it seemed more like a prison, and she alone was holding the key.

I inched across the carpet to her bedside, kneeling down to bring my face level with hers. She was so close to me, her warm breath caressing my cheeks. In life, I would've scooped her in my arms, ran my fingers through her silky raven hair, coaxing her to sleep with the lullaby I'd sung a thousand times before. She used to yearn for my voice. Plead for it. My only prayer now was that it would reach her as it did back then.

"Dani...I'm here," I whispered. "Open your mind and listen."

Her breathing steadied, eyes coming into focus as she stared right through me. I stiffened up, surprised to see her actually respond. She reached for the chain necklace hanging around her neck, fingering its circular gold pendant—a coin engraved with a compass rose. It was one of the few trinkets I'd gifted her before passing from the mortal realm. My last, to be specific. She clutched it tightly, raising it to her lips.

"Abuela...I miss you so much," Dani muttered to herself. "Are you still watching over me? Did you keep your promise?"

"Yes! Yes, of course I did," I said, leaning closer. "I never left you, mi amor. Not even for a moment."

Dani's eyes began to moisten with fresh regret. "Why is all this happening to me, Abuela? I tried to do everything right. I tried to open up like you taught me, but it only made things worse. Nobody wants me. Why should they? I hurt people. I hurt my dad. I'm angrier than ever and I don't know why."

I instinctively lifted my hand, gently stroking her forehead, my fingers passing through her skin without a hint of resistance. "Shhhh...that's the darkness talking, mi amor. Don't lose yourself staring inward. Look up and around you for love and wisdom. Look to your parents. Look to your Father in Heaven."

"I feel so alone," Dani continued. "I try to pray, but it doesn't seem like God hears me. Nobody does." She blinked back her tears, wiping her face with her pillow. "I don't even know if *you* can hear me."

My heart dropped to the floor, shattering to pieces. I was only inches from my beloved granddaughter, but never in my afterlife had I felt so incredibly far away. Other guardians had told me stories about this. How their precious family had strayed from the light. How they'd screamed into the void, begging for the other side of mortality to hear logic and reason only to fall on deaf ears. I thought Dani and I were beyond that, too strong to fail, yet here we were, and it couldn't be more terrifying.

"Dani, don't shut me out!" I cried. "I'm here! All of us are here! You just have to quiet your mind and let us in!"

The girl knitted her brows, sniffling softly, then tucked away the pendant of my necklace in her shirt. "I guess I really *am* alone."

She might as well have slugged me in the face. I floated backward onto my feet, fighting back tears of my own as I retreated out of the room into the hallway. How was this possible? Twelve years we'd spent, inseparable, basking in the joy of mutual companionship, and in a single day, a single *act*, Belial had thrown it all to the wind. Was my confidence an illusion from the beginning?

I trudged into the living room, peering over at the kitchen table to find Carmen sitting by herself, scrolling through the messages on her phone. Tulio and Kemuel had both vanished entirely. The excitement from earlier must have taken its toll. Laila waved to me out of the corner of my eye, seated on the edge of the couch with an expectant look.

"Any luck?"

I shook my head, wringing the sleeve of my robes in shame.

Laila glanced down at my forearm, noticing the lengthy gash from my battle at the cafeteria. The wound had already begun to close itself, no longer bleeding golden dust, but it was still clearly visible against my otherwise perfect skin. "Ven aquí, chica. Lemme have a look at that," she said, extending her hand.

I was never a fan of being coddled. Not by her, or anyone else for that matter. It made me feel weak. Incompetent. Then again, who was I to argue that right now? My day was a total failure. It would've been more fitting to simply hide up on the roof and sulk until morning, but the dull throb in my arm convinced me to reconsider. I settled onto the cushions beside Laila, begrudgingly offering my wounded limb.

"Ooooh, this was a nasty one," she said, inspecting it with interest. "An axe chop?"

"A whip lash," I replied flatly.

"Yup, that'll do it." Laila placed her other hand over the cut, squinting in concentration. After a few seconds, my arm began to tingle and glow, bright orange light erupting from within as though my bones had become a miniature sun. The pain instantly melted away, replaced by an invigorating warmth. It crept up my shoulder into my chest, enveloping me, purging me of all sadness and guilt. Then, just as I thought I'd returned to Heaven's bosom, it was gone. Laila withdrew her hand, revealing a flawlessly healed arm. "There we are. Good as new."

I clenched a fist, testing my rejuvenated muscles. They were springy and more responsive than ever, but even so, I couldn't bring myself to smile.

"What is it?" Laila asked, sensing the dark cloud looming over me.

I swallowed hard, glaring down at the floor. "What am I going to do, Laila? This new evil...I'm up against El Pecado de Ira. One of the seven most powerful diablos in Hell. How do I beat something like that? I can already feel Dani slipping away. My strength is fading along with her. What if he wins? What if I lose her to the darkness?"

Laila scooted closer, her voice calm yet scolding. "Why is it you keep talking as if this only concerns you? This is *our* household, *our* family at stake here."

"Yes, but Dani is *my* responsibility. The fate of her soul depends on me."

"Only you?" Laila snatched up her long braid of hair, menacingly twirling it with her fingers. "Tell me, Sarai, what's the greatest difference between the forces of light and the forces of shadow?"

I narrowed my eyes at her braid, knowing full well the punishment for answering wrongly. "Go ahead. Shower me with your wisdom."

"It's unity," Laila replied. "Evil fights only for itself. It devours everything else in pursuit of power, including its own. But light? We're the polar opposite. We fight for each other. All of us are pointed towards one goal. One family. One Father. Have you forgotten where your strength comes from in the first place?"

"Wait, you expect me to rely on other angels?" I tittered softly at the idea. "Sure, you and Kemuel are great, but have you seen what I have to work with out there? Those slackers are careless and complacent, indulging human fears of judgment and rejection. We're supposed to be on a higher plane of existence, inspiring our mortals to do the same. It's no wonder kids today are floundering. The diablos are running rampant while we simply bow down to the onslaught. Don't fool yourself, amiga. Nobody's coming to our rescue."

"How else do you think you're going to take down Belial?" Laila retorted.

"I need to find a way to get stronger. I need a power like Ethan's."

"Ethan?"

I winced, struggling not to blush. "He's one of the angels from school."

Laila raised an eyebrow. "Handsome?"

"Uuuhhhh...he's passable."

"That good, huh? Is he single?"

"Maybe you should ask him yourself."

"Maybe I will," Laila said, folding her arms. "He shouldn't be too hard to find. I'll just look for the guy who makes steam come out of your ears."

"Ha ha," I shrugged. "*Anyway,* when we were fighting back at the cafeteria, he was able to create a spirit projection I've never seen before. It wasn't merely a weapon. It was an entire suit of armor with a big fancy shield and sword. I wonder if I could replicate something like that."

Laila gently shook her head. "Wishful thinking, chica. I already told you that's not how spirit weapons work."

"Remember when we thought I could only generate one sword but then I made two? Maybe it's the same sort of deal. If I concentrate hard enough—"

"You were *always* able to make two swords," Laila cut in. "Spirit weapons are the reflection of a person's true nature. An extension of our will and demeanor. It doesn't matter if you're angel or demon, the result is always the same. Ranged weapons represent caution, precision and calculation. Axes and hammers are for those that favor brutality and dominance. Most angels use a single sword because of its balance of attack and defense. In your case, dual blades reflect speed, aggression and the ability to focus on multiple issues at once."

"Then what about Ethan?" I demanded. "Why does he get a sword, shield *and* a shiny set of duds?"

Laila stroked her chin, thoughtfully gazing up at the ceiling. "It's hard to say without knowing him personally, though I suspect he has a more protective instinct."

"What? I can be protective. Way more protective than *he* is. I wouldn't let Dani eat Funyuns until she was twelve."

"That's definitely true," Laila said, giggling into her hand, "but there's a bit more to it than that. A shield would suggest a passive style of defense. Very different from your, shall we say...smothering tactics. Our life experiences play a role as well. That armor of his must be a key part of his mortal identity."

I sank back against the couch, grinding my teeth. "Smothering...I'm not smothering. *You're* smothering..."

Laila smiled, placing her hand on my shoulder. "Listen, chica, I know it doesn't seem fair. I always thought it'd be cool to summon a bazooka, but instead, my talent lies in healing. We don't get to choose the gifts we're given. That's Father's job. Ours is to simply make the most of the ones we have."

I regarded the angel for a moment, marveling at how much she reminded me of Carmen. Not just because of her looks. That was a given for identical twins. Rather, it was that maternal insight. Like an anchor in the middle of a storm, firm and grounded, tugging me back to where I'm supposed to be with equal force. The epitome of need over desire. Laila was as much a rock for me as Carmen was for Daniela.

"How did you get so smart?" I said, grinning back at her. "You never saw a day of school in your life."

Laila chuckled, glancing over at Carmen. "I may have only had a ten-minute head start into this world, but that still makes me a big sister, and just because I died four hours after that, it doesn't mean I get to slack off either. My duty is to guide and protect. Even if it came through second-hand experience, every scraped knee, every broken heart, every crushing failure was a chance for me to learn and grow. It gave me the knowledge to help Carmen get stronger as well, gradually making us immune to the wiles of Inferno. You have to do the same for Daniela. And remember, our influence isn't confined to mortals alone. The spirits around you are starving for an example to follow. If they won't stand together against the darkness, then show them the way as I've done for you."

"You make it sound so easy," I said, pensively staring off into the distance. "I don't know the first thing about leading people. I just bark at them and they usually do what I say. How did I live so long and still come out of mortality feeling so clueless?"

"To be fair, I've been dead a lot longer than you," Laila replied. "Amazing what you can do without work and sleep to get in the way. But don't sell yourself short. Tulio is living proof of what a magnificent family you raised."

I turned to Laila, shaking myself from my trance. "How is he, by the way? He must have left the table in a hurry."

Laila nodded with a frown. "Another coughing fit. Probably spurred by all the drama. Kemuel went to watch over him while he rests."

"Figured as much. I think I'll go give Kemuel a break. Thanks for fixing the arm."

I rose from the couch, bidding my friend a grateful salute before stepping through the nearby wall. Wood and insulation flashed in front of me, giving way to the open dimness of the master bedroom. Tulio was already asleep under the covers, illuminated by the faint flicker of the TV mounted in the opposite corner. A silicone mask covered the lower half of his face, his CPAP machine hissing rhythmically with each rise and fall of his chest.

Kemuel hovered in the air beside the bed, sitting with legs crossed and eyes closed as though deep in meditation. If I wasn't already familiar with the gentle giant, his hulking form and fiery red mohawk would've been incredibly jarring.

"Good evening, Kemuel," I said, reverently creeping up to the bed. "Sorry I didn't greet you properly before. Everything's been so loco since we got home."

The angel didn't respond, his eyes still shut tightly.

"I take it things went smoothly with Scarvin today?"

Silence.

"AHEM," I said, pretending to clear my throat.

"Welcome, sister. Have you come to brighten your aura? Even in holy rest, one must endeavor to sharpen the mind." Aside from his lips, Kemuel hadn't moved a muscle.

"How's my son?" I asked, nodding to Tulio. "Laila tells me he had another episode."

"His spirit is strong," Kemuel replied, "but his flesh grows weaker by the day. The end of his earthly sojourn is fast approaching."

I reached for Tulio's hand, willing myself tangible enough to feel it. "Could you give us a few minutes?" I whispered.

"As you wish." Kemuel opened his eyes, unfurling his legs to touch down on the floor. He gave me a stoic but acknowledging look, then turned and vanished through the adjoining wall.

Alone at last, I squeezed my son's hand a little tighter, leaning forward to study his face. "Hola, Mijo...mama's here now. Everything's going to be okay..."

I listened to Tulio breathe, watched his eyelids flutter, wondering what it was he was dreaming about. A memory of me, perhaps? His childhood? Growing up in the house his father had built for us? I let myself slip into that same illusion, imagining my little boy tucked snugly in bed. My fingers gently stroked his cheek, prompting a sweet smile, and with a deep breath of my own, I started to sing. A spell woven especially for him. A charm of protection. A chant of affection. A promise that the next time he woke, the world would somehow be new.

Chapter 5

THE RENDEZVOUS POINT

ALL MORTAL EYES WERE ON DANI as she trudged into first period. Some followed her with a fearful curiosity. Others, like those of Candace and her crew, burned with a seething hatred. Even Mr. Elliot, who had arrived early with his mug of hot cocoa, stood watching in silence behind his podium until she'd taken her seat next to Hector.

As for the spiritual half of the class, it was Belial who stole the show. His enormous stature and commanding presence seemed to shrink the already crowded room. Demons raced to greet him, pushing and shoving each other, trampling the poor angels unfortunate enough to have been idling along the front row of desks.

Ethan waved from the other side of the stampede, gesturing for me to come over with a nervous smile. It was nice to see at least one supporter of my own, though my thoughts immediately flashed to the conversation I'd had with Laila the night before.

I nonchalantly checked to make sure steam wasn't coming out of my ears, then pushed off the ground into the air. None of the demons bothered to notice or care, too enthralled with the Sin of Wrath as I floated over their heads and touched down gracefully beside Daniela.

"Good morning, Milady," Ethan said, offering a bow. "How have you been holding up in the wake of yesterday's ordeal?"

I pursed my lips. "Could be better. A lot better. Dani's still pretty shaken up, and judging by the gauntlet of stares, everybody else is too."

"Indeed. Hector spent quite a while trying to defend your charge's honor, but the opposition was fierce. Candace wields a formidable army, and he now finds himself torn between social circles."

I glanced down at the drummer boy, watching as he tried to sneak eye contact with Dani. That coward. If he truly sympathized with her, why not say so? All it would take is a brief "I'm sorry that happened" or "Candace was way out of line." But he was just like all the others, happy to be a friend until he's needed the most.

"It's awfully hard to go where you want when you're hiding inside the herd," I said coldly.

Ethan sheepishly scratched his head. "I...I've been striving to help him with that. Having courage, I mean. It's a difficult thing to build...and so easily shattered. An angel's voice can only travel so far."

"You're preaching to the choir," I said, putting my hands on my hips. "Belial's got such a tight grip over Dani, she can barely hear me at all anymore."

"Is there anything I can do to help?"

I quickly shook my head. "This isn't your problem. It's mine. One way or another, I'll think of something."

"Alright, ladies and gents, playtime's over," Mr. Elliot said, taking a sip of his cocoa. "Everybody crack open your textbooks to page ten and let's get started. Who can read for me in their best monotone…?"

Belial and the other demons paused for a moment, realizing class was now in session, then shrugged their shoulders and went back to prattling amongst themselves. Since the kids were about to fall asleep with their eyes open, I suppose there wasn't much else for us to do. I sat myself in the air and crossed my legs, mulling over Laila's words of advice when somebody's finger poked me in the back.

I whirled around in a heartbeat, instinctively calling forth one of my swords only to find Beth's angel standing behind me. He held his hands up in surrender, the tip of my blade hovering just beneath his freckled nose.

"Peace be unto thee!" the angel gasped. "I mean thee no harm."

I shot Ethan a sideways glance, silently asking what to make of my new red-headed stalker.

Ethan froze, blinking at me with equal confusion.

"Your name. It's Malachi, right?" I said, turning back to the angel.

He slowly nodded with a hard swallow. "Aye. The very same."

I lowered my sword, dissipating it in a burst of light. "Was there something you needed, amigo? In case you hadn't noticed, yesterday's free-for-all has me a little on edge."

Malachi relaxed his arms. "My apologies. I was merely inquiring if thou wouldst speak with me privately."

"State your intentions," Ethan said, butting in. "It isn't becoming for a servant of Heaven to act so clandestinely."

I noticed his voice was suddenly deeper than usual. No. It couldn't be. Was he actually *jealous?* What was the deal with me and these old-school Shakespearian types?

"It's okay," I said, waving Ethan aside. "We've both seen Carrot Top in action. He couldn't hurt a flea."

Malachi winced, unsure how to take the comment. "Uuuuhh...thanks?"

"After you, amigo."

Ethan watched reluctantly as the angel and I made our way towards the back of the room, stopping in front of Beth's desk. The girl had her head propped on an elbow, staring at her open textbook while her monkey-sized demon peered at me from atop her shoulder. He hissed in disdain, then leaned up against his mortal to continue whispering something in her ear.

"Friendly little rodent, isn't he?" I sneered.

Malachi frowned with a sigh. "Pay him no heed. Snipes is entirely without manners."

"Fine by me." I folded my arms, studying the angel intently. "So, that dialect of yours. It's definitely ancient, but your sword skills are not. You're an Unborn, aren't you? And from the sound of it, fresh out of Heaven, no less."

"Tis true," Malachi replied. "I have yet to experience mortality. This is my first tour as a guardian, however, as thou art privy, I seem to be fumbling in that regard."

"Don't be so hard on yourself. Guiding souls to the light is a tough job."

Malachi's jaw tightened. "So I see. I wanted to properly thank thee for yesterday's rescue. Who knows what sort of ill fate would have befallen Beth and me hadst thou not intervened."

I looked away, trying to play it cool. "It was nothing, really. I'm sure you would've done the same for me."

"And I intend to," Malachi said, squaring his shoulders. "If ever thou art in need of aid, thou haveth my sword."

"Thanks, Aragorn. I'll keep that in mind."

The angel wrinkled his forehead. "Ara...who?"

"Don't worry about it, hermanito."

"Herma...nito?"

I cupped a hand over my mouth, stifling a chuckle. "Wow, you really are wet behind the ears, aren't you?"

He recoiled in surprise, running his fingers up the back of his neck.

"Listen, Malachi, I appreciate the offer," I said, pulling his hands down. "It's great that you want to lend me your strength, but I think Beth needs your attention a lot more than I do right now. She doesn't seem to be meshing with the other kids."

Malachi's expression sagged. "Aye. Despite her desires to, Beth has always struggled to converse freely with others. Years of homeschooling have left her isolated, and her parents' insistence on simple, modest attire has drawn scrutiny from her new peers. To make matters worse, that infernal beast, Snipes, continually worms his way into her mind, proclaiming that everyone despises her for being different."

"Well, I certainly know a thing or two about obnoxious diablitos," I said.

Malachi narrowed his eyes. "If only there was a mortal willing to put aside their apprehensions and extend the hand of friendship. Someone with the courage to prove Snipes wrong and dispel Beth's paranoia once and for all."

I glanced down at the floor, wishing I had a solid answer to his predicament. Dani was my obvious first resort, but she was already drowning in her own self-turmoil. There was Hector, but he didn't even have the stones to talk to the girl sitting right beside him. Everyone was divided by an invisible barrier, too worried about the perception of others to do what was necessary. The sheer absurdity of it all. I wanted to slap them upside the head and scream how childish the whole thing was. As I wrestled with the idea of following through, a voice began to call from above, whispering my name.

"Sarai...psst...Sarai, up here."

"Father?" I lifted my gaze, jerking backward in shock as I noticed a pair of faces poking through the panels in the ceiling.

"Guess again," Javan said with a wide grin. "We didn't see you get to campus this morning. Been looking everywhere for ya."

"Thank goodness you're okay," Ariel chirped, quivering excitedly beside him. "After what happened at the cafeteria, we thought Belial might've ripped you to shreds."

"Not yet," I said, clicking my tongue.

"Do you have a second to chat?"

"Hold on, let me check the queue." I twisted around to consult Malachi, flicking my eyes up at the ceiling. "You mind?"

"Oh, not at all," he replied. "Please, consort at thy leisure."

I turned back to Javan and Ariel, letting out a sigh as their faces withdrew into the fiberglass tiles. A gentle push of my toes sent me drifting after them, passing through the classroom's material canopy into the daylight of a blue open sky. The two angels stood waiting anxiously on the rooftop, its flat layer of stone granules glistening brightly under their sandaled feet.

"Okay, guys, here I am. What's up?"

"How are you so calm right now?" Ariel asked, running up to clutch my hands. "The Demon of Wrath is in our school! His followers are going crazy! I'm still having panic attacks over the riot he started!"

"Heh. I wasn't scared," Javan chimed in. "I just darted to the exit and waited for my boy, Alex, to catch up. He didn't care about getting drenched in apple sauce. It's one of his favorite foods."

Ariel tightened her grip on me, practically snapping my fingers. "But what about all the angels that got dusted? It'll take them weeks to regenerate up in Heaven. If I hadn't hidden myself under the salad bar, those monsters would have gotten me too!"

"Believe it or not, that wasn't my first rodeo," I said, yanking my hands from her grasp.

"But what if it happens again? What if they find me? Have you ever been slain before?"

"Stop being such a baby," Javan grunted. "I've been dusted plenty of times. It only hurts for a second. This one time, I got a spear shoved right up my—"

"No, I've never fallen in battle," I interrupted, "and there's no reason any of us have to start now."

"Wha...what do you mean?" Ariel whispered.

I furrowed my brow, straining to channel my inner Laila. "Are we not soldiers of Heaven? Did we not vow to protect our assigned mortals? Just because the diablitos struck first doesn't mean we're helpless. I took down several of them myself. If they try to rise against us, we need to stand together. Fight as one. Even the great and terrible Sin of Wrath isn't invincible."

"You sure about that?" Javan replied. "I saw you take a swing at him when he was messing with your human. Your blade didn't even break the skin. He caught it midair and threw you like a sack of potatoes."

My cheeks burned with embarrassment. "I...th-that was a...he got lucky is all. I just need to follow through a little harder next time."

Javan shook his head. "Sorry, Sarai, but it's no use. Even if you could hurt him, I overheard the other demons saying it would only make him stronger. His power comes from rage, and any pain you inflict would become his fuel."

"Sooooo, what, I'm supposed to simply give up? Cut my losses and surrender Dani to the fires of Inferno? I can't do that.

I'll *never* do that. We have to fight back. At the very least, we have to try."

Ariel stepped forward, gently grabbing me by the shoulders. "Sarai...I know how hard it must be to accept your limitations. I wish there was something I could do, but I'm a lover, not a fighter. I wasn't built for this kind of confrontation."

I wrenched myself away from her, snarling in disgust. "You...you *cowards!* Where is your faith? Where's your loyalty and compassion? We were sent here to guide souls back to the Father, not pal around and hide from the darkness. You aren't worthy to call yourselves guardians. You barely deserve to call yourselves angels. If you're not willing to fight for what you love, then you don't love anything at all."

Ariel shrank backward, retreating to Javan's side, tears stinging her eyes as he went to comfort her.

"Come on, Ari. We should probably go," he said, glaring at me.

"Yeah, you should," I barked at them. "Scamper away with your tails between your legs. It's what you're best at."

The two angels turned to leave, tossing me one last wounded glance before levitating off the roof into the sky. They descended over the far end of the school, disappearing behind a line of trees. All the while, I stood there, grinding my teeth, wondering if I'd gone too far. What else could I have done? My rant was harsh, but it came from a place of desperation, and more importantly, it was the truth. It *needed* to be said.

"You can't vanquish fear with your own rendition."

I spun around to find the upper half of Ethan's body protruding from the roof. He had his arms crossed, lips curled in disapproval. "*Qué es esto?* Have you been spying on me?"

"Let's call it, 'commiserating from afar.'"

"Not far enough."

Ethan rose from the shiny gravel, his tone blunted yet sympathetic. "You're a strong-willed guardian, Sarai. Nobody doubts that, but there's a difference between independence and stubbornness. Only a blind man would fail to see you've been pleading for help all morning. Don't be offended when someone answers the call."

Great. Now it was *my* turn to get smacked by the truth.

"What's the point?" I muttered. "Javan was right about Belial. He's out of my league. Sure, you and Malachi could help me gang up on him, but he's got friends too, and a whole lot more of them. Even if by some miracle we were to win, he'd simply regenerate and take his revenge on me when I'm alone. Somehow, I have to get more powerful. I have to be able to keep him in check no matter the circumstances."

Ethan stroked the stubble of his chin, pacing around me in a circle. "I'm not exactly certain how much stronger we could make you, but there's more than one way to cripple a demon."

"What do you mean?"

"Mortals aren't the only ones that are susceptible to temptation," he replied. "Wrath. Envy. Lust. Gluttony. Our enemies share these weaknesses as well. Some sins are more debilitating than others, but there's one that every single demon has in common."

"Pride."

"Precisely," Ethan nodded. "It was the very reason they were cast out of Heaven. With the right amount of cunning, it can be an incredible weapon."

"Not bad," I said, tilting my head with intrigue, "but it's not like I can flatter Belial into submission."

Ethan wagged a finger. "That's why our primary goal has to be Daniela. While every spirit has their own innate level of skill and strength, remember the true balance of power lies with their assigned human. The farther we can get Daniela from the darkness, the weaker Belial will become. Thanks to your diligence, she already has great potential for compassion and righteousness. If we could just remind her of who she really is, the scales would tip in your favor and bridge the gap between you and Belial."

"But that's the problem," I groaned. "She won't hear my voice."

"Then we'll have to find one she will," Ethan explained. "It's times like these when the only way to help a mortal is with another mortal. We have to employ Hector."

"Good luck with that," I said, rolling my eyes. "The spineless hedgehog can't even *talk* to Dani. How would we get him to offer any moral support?"

"His only issue is public opinion. If we could get them alone, one on one, somewhere Candace and her minions wouldn't interfere, then we might have a chance. We could use the choir room during lunch. It's a quiet place both of our humans are familiar with."

"What about Belial and your favorite succubus?"

Ethan bit his lip. "Yes...he and Jezazel could pose a problem, but I'm afraid this is as far as my thinking carries me. Any ideas?"

I took a deep breath and closed my eyes, playing through the whole scenario in my mind. A mortal advocate. A secluded rendezvous. A spiritual heart to heart. Father willing, this could actually work. All we needed to do was ditch the devils. But how? We couldn't use brute force. What were their weaknesses? Pride? Wrath? Envy? Then it hit me.

"I got it!" I shouted, triumphantly throwing my arms in the air.

"You do?"

I bobbed my eyebrows at Ethan, grinning from ear to ear. "Just leave it all to me. Promise you can get Hector to the choir room on time?"

Ethan smiled back at me, pressing a fist to his chest. "You have my word."

"Then it's a date."

I let myself slip through the roof into the classroom below, glancing over to check on Dani. She and the rest of her peers were still fighting to stay awake while the demons continued to crowd around Belial. Towards the edge of their huddle, I spotted my targets—Diva and Jezazel. They struggled to push their way closer to my beefy counterpart, calling out to him with little success.

Putting on my most cordial face, I sauntered up behind them, clearing my throat to get their attention. "Morning, ladies. Enjoying the view?"

Jezazel twisted her head around in a frightening one-eighty degrees. "Well, if it isn't Princess Prude. What do *you* want?"

"You've got a lotta guts showing your ugly mug around here," Diva said, looking me up and down in dismay. "Best watch yourself before we decide to finish what we started yesterday."

I kept smiling, completely undeterred. "You know, about that. I think we got off on the wrong foot. Let's clean the slate with a peace offering, shall we?"

Jezazel narrowed her sinister eye, rotating her body to face me. "Peace offering? What could you possibly have to offer us?"

I leaned in with a whisper, careful to make sure none of the other demons could overhear. "What would you say to a private audience with the Lord of Wrath?"

Dani strolled into the choir room with her lunch bag, relieved to find the chairs and stage totally deserted. She was never one to voluntarily chow down by herself, but with her recent fall from grace and the threat of Hurricane Candace lurking in the cafeteria, it didn't take much convincing. All I had to do was mention the safe seclusion of a place she used to love. And my favorite part? Belial didn't even bother to argue.

"I'm glad to see we're finally on the same page," he said, glancing around the studio. "This worthless girl doesn't deserve to eat with all the other brats. She needs to wallow in isolation. Let her hatred and resentment fester."

I turned away to hide my grin, whining in mock despair. "Oh no, not resentment. She needs peace and quiet to heal from her emotional wounds."

"Keep telling yourself that, short stack."

Dani slowly crossed the room, a glint of nostalgia in her eyes as she approached the tiered stands where the choir would sing. How many times had she been there before, harmonizing with her old friend Bonnie? For a moment, I worried the sight of it would evoke a fresh bout of pain, reminding her of happier days long gone, but instead, it brought a wistful smile to Dani's face. She seated herself on the lowest bench, settling in with her lunch when a couple of spirits crept through the nearby wall.

Diva and Jezazel, right on cue. They pointed and giggled at an unsuspecting Belial, giving themselves a last-minute primping before announcing their presence.

"Oh my Devil, is that the Lord of Wrath?" Diva said, acting surprised. "What a wild coincidence finding *you* here!"

Belial peered over his shoulder, his jaw hanging slack. "Aww, crap. It's those two."

"You're looking fabulously horrid today," Jezazel said, twirling a lock of her greasy black hair. "What's a hunky hellspawn like you doing in a place like this?"

I cringed at her pitiful excuse for a pickup line, almost choking out a laugh as she and Diva sashayed up to Belial. He shifted uncomfortably, nostrils flared, torn between his love for attention and the suffocating neediness of his fans.

"As you can see, I happen to be on the clock," Belial said, gesturing to Dani. "What exactly are *you* doing here?"

"The same thing everyone else is," Diva said, tracing a finger along his bulging pectorals. "Searching for a good time."

Belial's eyes fluttered ever so slightly. "Yeah, well, some of us actually take our jobs seriously. This kid's soul isn't going to condemn itself."

Jezazel pressed up against him, running her hand across his washboard abs. "Oh, come on," she croaked. "All work and no play makes Satan's proxy a dull boy."

"That's right," Diva added. "You deserve a well-earned break. We could get outta here, just the three of us. I know a sweet little frat house only a few blocks away. They party hearty 24-7. We could slip over there until lunch ends. Maybe possess a few drunken college kids and see where things go from there?"

Belial grinned, looking over to gauge my reaction.

"Don't you dare!" I cried dramatically. "Those poor innocent frat boys!"

The demon threw his head back with a cackle. "Ah, what the Heaven? A few minutes of playtime shouldn't hurt."

The succubi squealed with glee.

"That's the spirit!" Jezazel cheered.

"Let's go," Diva said, tugging Belial by the arm. "If we hurry, we can still catch the pledge week initiations."

The three of them took off into the air and vanished through the wall ahead, leaving me in silence next to Dani. She was none the wiser, munching on a sub sandwich of turkey and rye. Now that the riffraff were out of the way, all we needed was Hector. If Jezazel was here, he couldn't have been far. But where was he? Did Ethan seriously drop the ball after that valiant speech about helping me?

I tapped my sandal over the hardwood floor, debating whether or not to go looking for them. We wouldn't be able to get Dani another opening like this. If they didn't show up soon, I could lose my granddaughter forever.

Refusing to entertain the thought, I bolted for the door, about to step through it when its lever knob twisted from the other side. Daylight spilled over the floor, heralding the arrival of a teenage figure with his angel in tow.

"Sorry for the wait," Ethan said, flashing me his most dazzling smile. "The boy is far more bashful than he seems."

"Better late than never," I said, breathing a sigh of relief.

Dani lowered her sandwich, gaping in surprise. "Hector? What are you doing here?"

The drummer shuffled across the room, nervously scratching his head. "H-hey, Dani. I saw you rushing in the opposite direction of the cafeteria. Wanted to see if you were alright."

"You *followed* me?"

"Yeah...hope that's okay." Hector nodded to the section of bench beside her. "Mind if I join you?"

Dani shrugged, scooting over a smidge as he plopped down.

"Listen, I...I never got the chance to talk to you about yesterday," he said. "I'm so sorry about the way Candace treated you. It was really messed up."

Dani took a big bite of her sub and glared at the floor. "Maybe next time she'll think twice before picking a fight with me."

Hector cracked a mischievous grin. "That milk carton to the face was pretty epic. Serves her right. Did Kingsley throw the book at you?"

"She made me and Candace clean the whole cafeteria after school."

"Oooooh, that's harsh," Hector said with a wince. "Bet the two of you had fun with that."

Dani rolled her eyes. "Why didn't you ever tell me Candace was such a crazy witch?"

"The subject never really came up," Hector replied. "I knew she had an elitist attitude, but I've never seen her act that way before. Something about you really set her off."

Dani shook her head. "I'm not so sure it was me. Did you notice how toxic she got after noticing Beth? It was like that when we met in first period. Just mentioning Beth makes her go full Medusa. Why is that? Is it just because of how she looks?"

Hector pursed his lips. "I mean, don't we all pretty much judge people by how they look?"

"What, so if I was an ugly hobo, you wouldn't want to hang out with me?"

Hector paused, sensing the loaded question. "Um-mmm...no?"

"This boy's got a death wish," I chimed in.

To my astonishment, Dani chuckled at his honesty. "Fair enough," she said, quickly regaining her composure. "I get it. A person's outside can say a lot about their inside, but look at the ugliness that came out of Candace. Appearances can be deceiving, and we can't ever truly know someone if we aren't willing to give them a chance."

"I guess that's true," Hector mused. "People say Beth's weird and stuff, but as far as I can tell, she seems really nice."

I leaned close to Dani, focusing all of my will into a fervent whisper. "Maybe we should try reaching out to her."

Dani echoed me, her eyes widening as the idea took root in her mind. "Maybe we should try sitting with Beth during lunch. Give her some company for once."

"*We?*" Hector said, recoiling slightly.

"What's the matter? Too cool for that?"

"N-no...it's just..."

"Just what? You were willing to let *me* sit with you."

"Well, yeah, but we sit next to each other in class, so..."

"That's it?" Dani demanded. "You only talk to me because it's convenient?"

"No, it's...I..."

Ethan slid down onto the bench beside Hector, throwing an arm around the boy to offer his own words of encouragement. "It's okay, my friend. We're free from the prying gaze of your antagonists. Tell her how you really feel."

Hector wrung his hands, his voice trembling with sincerity. "From the moment I first saw you in here singing, I could tell there was something special about you, Dani. A sort of light in your eyes. The way you carry yourself. The passion you have for the things you do. I know it probably sounds super cheesy, but that's what drew me to you. I couldn't help wanting to be a part of it."

Dani gasped, her cheeks turning bright red. "Oh...uh...wow."

"*Ay, bendito,*" I said, reaching over to slap Ethan on the wrist. "You could've mentioned he had one of *those* waiting in the chamber."

The angel disarmed me with another one of his infernal smiles. "A man's heart can be a whimsical thing, Milady."

Hector rubbed the back of his neck, apparently lacking his guardian's more polished swagger. "Sorry to drop all that on you," he said to Dani. "It's hard for me to know when to pump the brakes sometimes, especially with how guarded people can be. I wish I could open up more often. I'm sure Beth would think so too, but everyone's always watching, judging our every move. All it takes is one bad image and you're an outcast."

"Like me?" Dani asked.

"No, that's not what I—" Hector tightly folded his legs, twisting sideways on the bench to face her. "Listen, you are *not* an outcast. Not unless you want to be. Sure, the food fight was a little over the top, but standing up to Candace was what really made an impression. You did something no one else has been brave enough to do. It makes them wonder if you're planning to tip the throne or compete for it yourself."

"What if it's neither? All I want to do is get along."

"I understand how you feel," Hector replied, "but it's not that simple. Choosing to be someone's friend will always make you someone else's enemy. Sooner or later, we all have to pick a side. You just have to try as best you can to pick the winning one."

"Even if it means joining a bunch of superficial vipers?"

Hector bit his tongue.

"I refuse to do that," Dani said softly. "I won't let jerks like Candace dictate who I can and can't be. You shouldn't either."

I beamed with satisfaction, shaking my fist in the air. "That's my girl!"

The percussionist hung his head, my granddaughter's words piercing him like a cold knife through the chest. There was no denying his own hypocrisy—the inner clash between doing what was right and what was easy. Which side would ultimately win? The shallow perception of all his peers, or the trust of a girl he'd barely met?

Hector couldn't feel it on his shoulders, but his angel tightened an arm around him, exuding a presence of warmth and peace. A tender assurance that he wasn't alone, regardless of his decision. It brought a subtle mist to his eyes, humbling him to the truth of his own weakness.

"I wish I was as strong as you," he whispered to Dani. "I wish it didn't matter so much what other people think."

She scooted closer, a knowing smile broadening as she pointed up at the ceiling. "My abuela used to say there's only one person whose opinion really matters. He's infinitely kind, wise, patient, and He created us in His image. Why should we care what the world thinks of us? I'll take Him over Candace any day."

"Well...when you put it *that* way," Hector chortled.

Dani leaned against him, playfully giving him a nudge. "So, where's your lunch, drummer boy? Did you already eat?"

He looked up, his stomach promptly growling in reply. "Yeeaaah, no," Hector said sheepishly. "I was planning to grab something from the cafeteria, but when I saw you in such a hurry, I..." His voice trailed off, spurring a renewed grin from Dani.

"Here," she said, breaking off the unbitten half of her sub sandwich. "Food's always better when it's shared." She handed him the turkey on rye, his face lighting up as though it was a bar of gold.

"Really? You sure?"

"Yup."

He graciously accepted the treasure, moaning with delight as he took his first chomp. As the two of them enjoyed their meal, Ethan motioned for me to come sit, a cheerful glow in his countenance.

"I must confess, Milady, this venture has proven even more profitable than I'd hoped."

"It's a good start," I said, settling down beside him. "We've won this first battle, but the war is far from over."

Ethan flexed his arms, their muscle structure looking slightly more defined than I remember. "I can already feel it," he said, squeezing his bicep. "Hector is growing closer to the light. It's bolstering my power. Do you feel it too?"

I closed my eyes for a moment, trying to sense if Dani had triggered any changes in my spirit. There was definitely an improvement since this morning, but nothing major. Nothing beyond what I had when Belial first arrived.

"It isn't enough," I replied. "I need a lot more to repel that brutish puerco." I turned to Ethan, swallowing my pride to feed my curiosity. "There's something I've been meaning to ask you about your spirit weapon. In the fight yesterday, you were able to summon more than just a sword and shield."

"You're referring to my armor?" Ethan deduced.

I nodded. "Please, tell me...how do you do it?"

He glared down at the floor, struggling to articulate his thoughts. "You're asking me how I breathe. How I blink. It isn't so much an action I perform. Rather, it's a part of me. An instinct, like a second skin when I need it most. The echo of what I felt the last time I donned my armor in mortality."

I shifted to the edge of my seat, lost in fascination. "What happened the last time you wore it?"

"I paid the ultimate price for disobedience," Ethan explained. "As I mentioned before, I was once a member of the Knights Templar, a military order tasked with securing and protecting the holy land of Jerusalem during the twelfth century. Several months after arriving there, my commander sent me with a small detachment to patrol the nearby villages. We'd received reports of banditry, and sure enough, discovered an army of marauders attacking one such town along the coast. Vastly outnumbered, our captain ordered us to retreat and seek reinforcements...but I refused."

"Why?"

"I couldn't simply leave those villagers behind," he continued. "They were being slaughtered. Kidnapped. Enslaved. Had I waited for reinforcements, the town would've long been burned to the ground, its every resident slain or captured. So I stayed to fight alone. To uphold my vow to protect the innocent."

"You fought an army *by yourself?*"

Ethan gave a half-nod. "I tried, using stealth and brutality to bring down their scouts. By midday, they'd begun to engage me in open battle, losing many to the edge of my sword, but by the time night had finally fallen, so did I, succumbing to my wounds."

"You failed?"

"I allowed more than half the villagers to escape from danger. True, some would have said I died in vain, but that's not how I see it. Even if I'd rescued only one solitary person, I consider my vow fulfilled. That's what it takes for me to summon my armor. It means reliving that moment of resolve, abandoning any sense of self to protect those around me."

I leaned forward in thought, resting my chin on my knuckles. "So, volunteering to cover me wasn't really an act of machismo after all," I concluded. "It's those kinds of situations that put you in your highest form. How amazing it must be to have the honor of knighthood ingrained in your soul."

"Each of us is blessed with unique talents," Ethan said, trying not to blush. "Just look at your superb sword skills and iron fighting spirit. I imagine you were quite the legend in your era. What was your profession? War chief? Counter-assassin?"

I tossed him a sideways glance, abruptly bursting into laughter.

"Bounty hunter, perhaps?"

I roared even louder, clutching my sides while he sat there in total confusion, awkwardly forcing himself to chuckle along. After finally getting it all out of my system, I wiped the tears from my eyes and panted the correct answer. "Try 'housewife,' amigo."

Ethan's jaw practically dropped to the floor. "*Housewife?* You must have had quite the rocky marriage."

"Not in the way you'd expect," I snickered. "Truth be told, most of my scrappiness comes from growing up with six older brothers. When every stick in the yard becomes a version of Excalibur, it's kill or be killed."

"Your brothers taught you how to slay people with dual blades?"

I shook my head. "All that stuff came after I died. My son's guardian, Kemuel, was an actual war chief in his time. He swore off violence before passing on, but with some coaxing, he agreed to teach me how to defend myself against demonic incursions."

"Remarkable." Ethan regarded me, impressed with my credentials. "I have to say, given how cold you are to the other angels, I'm surprised you were able to make such a capable friend."

"It isn't about being cold," I shrugged. "It's about having standards. Growing up in Puerto Rico, I learned pretty quickly that if you wanted to survive, the only one you could depend on is yourself. Trust is a hard-fought commodity, and even in the afterlife, people are careless and foolish. Relying on them for matters of eternal consequence is a fast way to end up in a ditch."

Ethan's expression soured. "How tragic to wall yourself like that. It sounds as though you barely had the chance to live."

I furrowed my brow, staring through him into my distant past. "The problem is that I lived for too long," I muttered. "I watched the world slowly rot away over the years, greed and arrogance giving rise to war and famine. Hundreds of millions of souls falling to sin and indulgence, happily marching to Inferno without the slightest clue of what awaits them. That's why I'm so defensive. I can't let it happen to my family, and I'd sooner burn in hellfire myself before I entrust them to mediocre spirits."

"I understand your plight," Ethan said, placing his hand on my shoulder. "All the more reason not to burden yourself alone. As a man who died in solitude, believe me when I say there is power in numbers. Some things can only be achieved when we open up and choose to put our faith in others."

I rolled my eyes. "Now you're starting to sound like Laila."

"Laila?"

"My daughter-in-law's angel."

"What a beautiful name. Is she as charming as you are?"

"Oh, don't worry, I've got nothing on her."

Ethan grinned. "She must be exceedingly wise as well to have noticed the same flaws as I do."

"*Flaws?*" I growled. "Look in a mirror some time. You talk about vowing to protect the innocent, but you didn't lift a finger to help Beth yesterday."

"I sit before you to rectify that mistake," he replied. "Perfection is a journey, and everyone has something to repent of, Sarai. How about yourself?"

I recoiled in shock, opening my mouth to fire back when a voice suddenly boomed over the school's PA system. Principal Kingsley's. It was stern yet trembling with urgency.

"*Daniela Rivera, please come to the front office right away. I repeat, Daniela Rivera, grab your things and come to the front office immediately.*"

I froze, the decree sending a chill running down my spine. "No...it can't be. It's too soon..."

Dani exchanged glances with Hector, reaching into her pocket for her flip phone. It was customary for her to keep the ringer on vibrate while at school, but as she opened up a chain of unread text messages, her eyes widened in horror.

"*Dad....!*"

Chapter 6

HOMECOMING

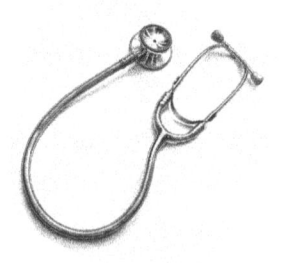

DANI AND HER MOM raced down the hall, Laila and I hot on their heels as a nurse directed them to a set of double doors. They burst on through, feet pounding against the shiny tiles, disrupting the quiet sterility of the hospital's emergency wing.

Where was he? Where was Tulio? I wanted to be the voice of reason, of comfort, assuring my granddaughter that everything would be alright. But how could I? I had no way of knowing. It wasn't possible for an angel to lie. All I could think of was finding him. My little boy.

As we rounded the next corner, I spotted another spirit rushing toward us. A demon with a single broken horn.

"Scarvin! What happened to Tulio?" Laila cried.

"He had another coughing fit and collapsed in the kitchen," the imp said, jogging alongside us. "Fortunately, he was able to dial 911 before going unconscious. Ambulance got here about an hour ago." Scarvin glanced over his shoulder, scanning the empty corridor behind me. "Where's Belial?"

"Probably still wandering the school looking for us," I replied. "And Kemuel?"

"Never left Tulio's side." Scarvin slowly trailed from the group, calling after me with a hand cupped to his mouth. "Better hurry, Sarai. And for what it's worth, I'm sorely going to miss him…"

"Over there!" Carmen pointed to a woman standing with a clipboard at the end of the hall. Judging by the white lab coat and stethoscope around her neck, she must have been one of the doctors. Behind her was a sliding door large enough to fit a gurney, the words "intensive care" painted above it. She looked up as we came stampeding over, raising a hand to stop us.

"Are you Mrs. Rivera?" she asked with a blank expression.

"Yes," Carmen answered breathlessly. "Where's my husband? Is he alright?"

The doctor glanced between her and Dani, a somber tone in her voice. "I'm going to need you to stay calm and listen very closely to what I'm about to tell you," she said. "The inflammation in your husband's lungs has gone critical. We've tried giving him corticosteroids to bring it down and open up his bronchioles, but his body isn't responding to the treatment. In his current state, it's only a matter of time before his lungs are no longer able to absorb sufficient oxygen."

"W-w-wait," Carmen gasped. "What are you saying?"

"I'm sorry, Mrs. Rivera…your husband's dying," the doctor replied. "We've done everything we can to make him comfortable, keep his airway as clear as possible, but his vital organs have already started to shut down. I'll have the nurses give you some time to say your goodbyes."

Carmen stared at her, utterly numb with denial. Dani shared the same horrified look, too shocked for the pain of reality to sink in. They just stood there in silence as the medical staff vacated the room ahead, only stepping forward after Laila and I placed a hand on their backs.

The distant echoes of the corridor quickly faded away, drowned beneath a medley of beeps and whirs coming from the machinery inside. Monitors flickered beside the bed with bright lines and numbers, time slowing to a crawl as Tulio came into view. He lay propped up in the pale fluorescent light, trembling, rasping with each labored breath of the oxygen cannula hanging from his nostrils. His hand slid feebly over the bed's plastic side rail, reaching for his wife and daughter as he quietly forced a whimper from his throat.

"My girls..."

Kemuel's towering form stood in the far corner, still as a statue, watching in silent reverence as the mortals rushed to Tulio's side. Dani collapsed onto her knees, clutching his hand, tears welling in her eyes at the sight of her father's anguish.

"I'm sorry," he whispered between gasps. "I thought we'd have...a few more nights together."

"Don't talk like that," Dani said, lips quivering. "You're gonna get better, Dad. You always get better."

"Mija..." Carmen put her hand on Dani's shoulder, choking back a sob. "You heard what the doctor said. We all knew this was going to happen eventually."

The girl frantically shook her head. "No...not yet. We're not ready...I'm not ready..."

Tulio smiled weakly, trying to interrupt. "Mi amor..."

"You just have to be strong, Dad. Give the medicine a chance to work."

"Please...listen..."

"We're gonna leave here together, you'll see. I'll make your favorite dinner and—"

"Dani."

Tulio squeezed her hand as hard as he could, the sound of her name finally catching her tongue. She couldn't hold back the dam any longer, grief streaming down her face as the truth became inescapable.

"I love you so much," he whispered. "Both of you are my everything...but God's calling me home, Mija. It's time for me to see your abuela again."

Carmen added her hand to his and Dani's, swallowing the lump in her throat. "Papi...thank you for always being my light in the darkness...for making me laugh when all I wanted to do was cry. We really did have a great run, didn't we?" She tittered softly, her voice breaking as she gazed into his eyes. "My heart was always yours, Papi. No matter where we go, it always will be."

Tulio nodded, tears dripping from his oxygen tubes onto the thin white bed sheets below. "I didn't deserve you," he replied, "but you never gave up on me. Either of you. It brings me so much peace to know how strong you are."

I knelt down beside Dani, wrapping my arms around her, trying to amplify the comfort in her father's words, but there was a deep agony swelling inside her. A searing regret for the person she was not a day before.

"I'm so sorry," she bawled. "I didn't mean it. All those terrible things I said to you. That you didn't care. That I didn't need you. Any of it." Dani hunched over, desperately pressing Tulio's knuckles to her forehead. "I need you now more than ever. You're supposed to be there when I graduate. You're supposed to walk me down the aisle at my wedding. You have to see the restaurant we open together. Grow old with mom. You can't go, Dad. Please, don't go. I'm so sorry."

"Mija..." Tulio pulled her close, gently stroking her head. "None of us are ever truly gone," he purred. "Not with a love like this. Promise me you'll keep it alive. Share it with those around you."

Dani lurched forward, burying her face in his hospital gown. "I...I'll try..."

Carmen joined in as well, encircling them with a tender embrace. I could only imagine how much she didn't want to let go of that moment, clinging to the faint hope that if she could just hold on a little longer, divine powers would intervene and restore her husband's vitality. After all, wasn't that what she believed in? An all-powerful God of mercy?

But Tulio was right. The bell had been rung. Rivers of sorrow stained Carmen's cheeks as she heard his breathing slowly grow heavier. A shiver ran through his body, intensifying into a fully-fledged seizure.

"Dad?" Dani pulled away, terror washing over her as she watched his eyes roll backward, fluttering violently.

"Help! Doctor, we need help!" Carmen lunged for the emergency call button beside the bed, mashing it repeatedly with her finger.

Nurses flooded the room, the woman in the white lab coat rushing up behind them. She scanned the readouts on the medical equipment, firing off a string of commands.

"Sorry, Mrs. Rivera, but it's time for you to go. Gene, please escort them out. Tess, get pulmonology in here *stat*. He's going into cardiac arrest. I need someone on vitals and EKG..."

A burly man in blue scrubs descended over my son's family, hastily trying to usher them out of the room. Carmen didn't resist, bidding Tulio farewell with one last tearful glance.

Dani was another story. She wrestled free of her escort, blinded by remorse, desperately fighting to break through the wall of nurses to reach her father. "No! Dad! Stay with me! I didn't get to say goodbye! Please, let me say goodbye!"

Two more staff members went to hold her back, gradually dragging her into the hallway. She continued to struggle, her wet eyes never leaving the hospital bed until the frosted glass door slid shut between them.

"I love you, Dad! I promise!"

Her voice faded into the distance, giving way to the panicked chaos of Tulio's final moments. I'd seen death so many times before, tasting its bitter cup for myself not too long ago, but to see Dani like that. Crushed. Distraught. It was more painful than taking my last breath. If only she were able to peer through the veil of mortality, beyond the shallow veneer of the physical world, and know with all surety that this wasn't the end. That life merely passes from one state to another.

I turned back to my son, approaching his bedside, ignoring the humans as they slipped mutedly in and out of my spirit. He was still writhing, suffocating, too frightened to let himself drift off to sleep. So I took my child's hand as I'd done the night he was born, closed my eyes, and started to sing.

The words caught in my throat at first, weighted by the memories of a small brick house on the fringe of an even smaller town. Our first home in California. A place of beauty and refuge. As the melody poured from my lips, I found myself standing in a darkened nursery once again, soft moonlight sneaking through the window to caress my little boy's face. He looked up at me with those big brown eyes, smiling sweetly as my voice, trembling and raw with emotion, chased away all his worries and fears.

I put every ounce of my soul into the chorus, raising a crescendo amidst the noise of shouting doctors and beeping machinery. The only thing that mattered was the baby in my arms, so tiny and frail. The greatest miracle my Father in Heaven had ever given me. I wrapped him in the warm tranquility of my song, the steady cadence of my heartbeat making his eyelids grow heavy.

Even as he fell quiet and still, his pulse dropping to a flatline, I couldn't bring myself to stop. There were too many precious words left unsaid. Too much love I'd failed to share while I was still flesh and blood. All of it cascaded from me now, an overwhelming torrent of days past and future. The summation of my earthly existence.

I don't recall exactly when the medical staff surrendered to the inevitable, silently filing out of the room in defeat. It must have been sometime between the final verse of my lullaby and the moment Tulio's spirit began to rise from his body. I simply remember holding that last unfettered note, wringing it for all it was worth when his voice called out to me in disbelief.

"Mama...?"

I opened my eyes, blinking away the tears to find him sitting up on the bed. His spirit was free of all its worldly tethers, no more tubes or wires, no shortness of breath, visually restored to his physical prime. His hospital gown was now a set of robes identical to mine, pure and white as the driven snow. He studied my face, weeping joyfully as I answered him with a fervent nod.

"Welcome to eternity, Mijo."

Tulio threw himself in my arms, hugging me tightly. "I missed you so much," he whispered in my ear. "You look so young...so beautiful..."

"Our spirits are ageless," I whispered back. "We're no longer bound by the limits of time and space, forever preserved at the peak of our form."

He rested his head against mine. "I was so scared, Mama. I didn't want to let go."

"It's okay, mi amor. It's over now," I said, running my fingers through his thick ebony hair. "Leave the pain and sadness behind. Let yourself embrace the light." We held each other for what felt like hours, forgetting about the other angels in the room until Kemuel stepped forward, cutting through the silence with his gravelly baritone.

"Forgive me, brother, but the kingdom of Heaven awaits your arrival. There is much for you to learn and see."

Tulio pulled away from me, reeling at the sight of Kemuel's mohawk and tribal markings. "Who...who are you?"

Kemuel raised his hands in front of him, bowing with a fist to his open palm. "I am he who has watched over you your entire life. The chosen guardian of your immortal soul."

"Don't worry," I said, giving Tulio's arm a reassuring squeeze. "He's one of us. An angel from above."

"A-a-an angel? From *above?*"

Kemuel nodded, offering the tiniest grin. "Indeed, brother. Come, let me show you the glory that lies beyond this fallen world."

He turned to the far wall and swiped his hand through the air, painting a trail of blinding light across its plain blue surface. The glowing streak began to widen and grow, expanding to create a circular portal. On the other side, towers of amber and crystal soon came into view, casting their shadows over Heaven's capitol—the Golden City. Its streets were teeming with other angels, all clothed in white vesture, bustling between buildings of glittering stone. The sky above was an aurora of otherworldly pastels, stars gleaming through the brilliance of a never-ending sunrise.

I'd only seen it once before. The day I died twelve years ago. It was only for a short time, my duties demanding a swift return to Earth, but the city was no less magnificent now than it was back then. I found myself gasping for breath, Tulio as well, a rapturous magnetism beckoning for us to enter the portal.

"Is that...Heaven?" Tulio whispered.

"It is," Kemuel said, extending his hand. "Come with me, brother. The Father awaits you upon His throne."

"M-me?" Tulio stammered.

"Yes, of course. Be not afraid. He joyfully greets all His children as they pass into eternity."

Tulio glanced down at his spiritual body, then back to his physical one—his empty chrysalis—slowly wrapping his mind around what was happening. Fear and doubt soon faded from his eyes, conquered by a blaze of renewed faith. He swung his legs over the edge of the bed, hoisting himself onto solid ground. His bare feet kissed the shiny tiles, his brows popping up at how spry and weightless he felt without the chains of gravity and arthritis.

"Mama, look at me!" Tulio cheered, twirling around in circles. "I'm light as a feather! My lungs are perfect again!" He took a few steps toward the portal, the most elated smile on his face until he realized I hadn't moved from beside the bed. "Mama...aren't you coming with me?"

I shook my head, fresh tears filling my eyes. "I can't, Mijo. Not yet."

"*What?* But why?"

"Daniela. When I was nearing the end of my mortal life, you brought her to the hospital for one last visit. I tried to explain to her that our paths were about to diverge, but the poor little girl simply couldn't understand. She couldn't bear the thought of never seeing me again, so I made her a promise. A vow to always watch over her. To always stay by her side...and I intend to keep it."

Tulio tightened his jaw, walking up to clutch me by the shoulders. "I had no idea. This whole time you've been..." His voice trailed off, a steely resolve creeping onto his face. "I want to stay here with you, Mama. My family still needs me."

I reached up, gently prying myself from his grip. "No, mi amor. You belong in the Golden City. Papa's waiting for you there. The rest of our family is too. Our ancestors. They have so much to teach you."

"But, Mama, please, Dani and Carmen—"

"Are in good hands," I said, gesturing to Laila behind me. "We'll bring them home when the time is right. Believe in me as I've done for you."

"But when will I see you again?" Tulio whimpered. "How will this ever be Heaven without you?"

I forced a comforting smile, brushing my fingers against his cheek. "Time and space are nothing but words to us now, remember? A cosmos between us...a few decades...all of it's less than a grain of sand in the ocean, mi amor. We'll be together again before you know it."

Tulio nodded reluctantly, choking out the only reply he could. "I love you, Mama."

"I love you too, Mijo," I whispered. "I always will."

Tulio leaned into my hand, savoring my touch a moment longer, then backed away, turning to the open portal. He straightened up, holding his head high, and with a deep breath, stepped through to the other side. Kemuel went to follow him, pausing to glance at me over his shoulder.

"Farewell, sister. May your aura always be bright and pure," he said solemnly. "Take care of Laila for me, and should the jaws of darkness gape wide to swallow you, remember the unquenchable power of Father's light."

I nodded, watching as he turned and led Tulio down a rocky hillside to the Golden City. The portal's luminous ring shrank and vanished in a burst of white embers, leaving me in the cold silence of the operating room with Laila and my broken heart. She inched up beside me, struggling to offer a nugget of consolation when I collapsed against her and began to weep.

"After all these years, he finally heard my voice. Saw my face. Felt my arms around him. So why do I feel so empty inside? Why does it still hurt so much knowing this wasn't truly goodbye?"

Laila didn't say a word. She simply held me, rubbing my back as drops of bittersweetness soaked into the folds of her robe.

Chapter 7

THE GREATEST TEACHER

A WEEK HAD COME AND GONE since Tulio's funeral, but the sting of his passing still lingered heavily in the air. An empty seat at the table. His various possessions scattered across the house. Every little thing, a constant reminder of the soul we were missing. The most jarring part was how the rest of the world simply kept on spinning, oblivious to our loss. I suppose I couldn't blame them. Death literally happens every single day, and as always, life has to go on. People have jobs to do. Responsibilities regardless of their emotional state.

Belial certainly didn't have a problem with that. Of course, he was a bit irked that he wasn't at the hospital to capitalize on Dani's pain, but that was the price of his fraternal debauchery, and once we finally got home, he went straight to work. Whispers of regret for how she'd treated her father, flooding her mind with scenarios of what she could've done but didn't. I tried to explain that there was no point in dwelling on the past. The only thing that truly mattered was the future, yet once again, my voice fell on deaf ears.

With Monday approaching, Carmen knew she'd have to return to her desk at the bank. She was now the family's sole provider, and that would mean coaching her daughter back into the normal routine as well. Dani hadn't been to school since that lunch with Hector, and though her mom offered more time for her to grieve, Dani insisted that she was ready. Hopefully, the drama from her first day of class would've subsided, making the transition a tiny bit easier.

So much for the optimism of youth.

The other kids stared in silence everywhere she went. Even Hector was barely able to muster a half-decent hello. Things were awkward when she was only a milk-chucking delinquent. But with her own father dying shortly after? The notably long absence? What could they possibly say to that? Sucks to be you? As far as anyone was concerned, my poor granddaughter was cursed.

Dani zombied her way through the first few classes, eventually traipsing into the cafeteria for lunch. She'd considered hiding in the choir room again, resigning herself to the asylum of isolation, but despite Belial's protests, she decided to go public. Maybe she figured it was the best way to prove she wasn't a crazy engine of destruction. If people could see her as another timid, unassuming teenager, perhaps they'd let her back into the fold. But where to sit?

Hector was in his usual spot at Candace's table, surrounded by a horde of flying monkeys in designer clothing and the wicked witch herself. He met Dani's gaze, bristling at the thought of what would happen if she tried to mingle with Candace again.

Reading his expression, Dani scanned the rest of the room. Beth Starkovsky was still sitting alone in the far corner. A fitting place for a fellow pariah, but Dani didn't seem willing to accept rock bottom just yet. Instead, she opted for the social middle ground, toting her sack lunch to the half-empty table of choir kids at the nearest edge of the cafeteria. I recognized a few of them from the previous year. Dani must have been banking on their familiarity to grant her safe harbor.

Most of them ignored her as she plopped down at the end of the bench, some throwing a cursory glance.

Dani knitted her brows, frowning at the cold reception. She hated being invisible.

Meanwhile, I was wishing I could take her place. With Belial's towering bulk at my side, every spirit in the room had their eyes glued to us, watching in fascination. The last time he and I were here together, total anarchy ensued. Was history about to repeat itself?

"Look at this pathetic meat bag," Belial said, gesturing to Dani. "Who told her she could eat with all the other brats? A dog should lick her slop off the floor." He peered across the cafeteria to the popular table, locking eyes with Diva. The succubus tossed her fiery blue hair, grinning flirtatiously as he flicked his chin at Candace.

I couldn't believe it. They were at it *again*. With Dani in her fragile state, it wouldn't take much for them to push her over the edge. One slap, one barrage of empanadas was all Candace needed to get her expelled or worse. I couldn't let that happen. Not while I was in one piece.

Diva bent down beside her mortal, the girl's face twisting maliciously as she whispered in her ear. Candace's scrawny angel, Abigail, leaned over the opposite shoulder, attempting to quash Diva's influence, but it was no use. Evil Barbie had been activated, her icy blue eyes fixing on Dani with a laser focus.

My heart sank, my mind racing for a way to stop them. I looked at Ethan. He was standing only a few feet behind Hector, catching sight of my desperation. Without me having to say a word, he lunged for his boy, ordering him to distract Candace. Hector clenched his fists, glancing between Dani and her rising antagonist, about to intervene when Jezazel jumped into the mix.

"Don't even *think* of moving a muscle," she hissed at the boy. "You really wanna end up like that loser, Beth? If you get in the way, every ounce of street cred you've earned over the last three years will be flushed down the toilet. What kind of girls do you think you'll score once you've been demoted from drumline captain to Ron Weasley?"

Hector froze, her threat successfully scaring him into hesitation.

"*Ay, bendito!* You have *got* to be kidding me!" I cried.

"Don't pay her any heed!" Ethan shouted over Jezazel. "Hermione is a worthy maiden!"

Dani looked up, bracing herself as she noticed Candace sauntering over from across the room. She could see the dark clouds gathering on the horizon. The only question was if she would run or try to weather the storm.

"Well, if it isn't our very own Iron Chef," Candace said, sliding backwards onto the bench beside Dani. "Did you have a nice vacation? We missed you soooo much."

Dani stared at her brown paper bag on the table, struggling to avoid eye contact. "Oh really?" she muttered.

"Why, of course, silly!" Candace gave her a slightly more than playful shove. "I've been dying to show my appreciation after you forced me to clean the entire cafeteria the other day. It was so much fun explaining to my dad why I came home three hours late with my outfit totally ruined."

Dani winced at the mock pleasantries in her voice.

"Hey, I've got an idea, Chef. How 'bout you buy me a new outfit and we'll put this whole spat behind us? We'll be bestest friends forever, mmkay?"

"Look, I don't want any trouble," Dani said softly. "You messed up my clothes too, so let's just call it even."

"*Even?*" Candace's eyes flashed, a heated barb slipping into her tone. "My tank top was an exclusive from *Zadig and Voltaire*. That means it was worth more than your entire existence. The least you can do is ask your daddy for some allowance to share, yeah?"

Dani tensed, the hairs on the back of her neck standing on end.

"Oh, that's right," Candace said, snapping her fingers with a grin. "He kicked the bucket, didn't he? How inconvenient."

The words tore open Dani's freshly bandaged wounds, her eyes turning red and moist with pain.

"It's strange how the old geezer shuffled off right after that debacle you caused. Almost like he couldn't handle the shame.

I mean, who would want to be the parent of such a disruptive poser? I'd probably want to keel over too."

"Shut up," Dani whispered. She grit her teeth, fingers quivering as they curled into a fist.

"Look on the bright side. At least now your mommy's free of that useless gas bag. She can go pimp herself out to some rich tycoon so you can afford to replace my outfit."

"*Shut up.*" It was louder this time. A menacing growl.

"What's the matter? Can't handle the truth?" Candace leaned closer, grinning into Dani's ear. "You gonna run home and cry some more? Go ahead. Cry yourself to sleep and don't ever wake up."

Belial threw his head back with a laugh. "Yeeeeesssss! That's it! Feel the rage bubbling inside you! Let the pressure build, higher and higher, then unleash it all at once!"

I threw myself onto the opposite side of the bench beside Dani, pleading with her as she slowly turned to Candace. "Don't strike her, mi amor, it's a trap! She wants you to do it! It'll give her the power to destroy you! Don't give in to your anger!"

"You know what you have to do," Belial said, placing his bear-sized claw on Dani's shoulder. "This blonde wretch deserves to be silenced. She disrespected your mother, even your dearly departed father. She needs to have her skull smashed concave. The world would be better off without her. They just lack the courage to follow through. Show them you're brave enough. Defend your honor by punching a hole through her blasted face!"

Dani's bicep tightened, her breathing heavy and ragged.

In that moment, despite the heightened panic coursing through me, a strange kind of serenity suddenly swept over my mind. A peaceful clarity that seemed to come from somewhere outside my own head, as though my spirit had left my body a second time. It reminded me of my son's final words to his daughter. A promise she willfully accepted.

"Dani..." Her name escaped my lips differently than before, infused with a soothing power. "Your papa loved you more than you could ever know. Is this how he would've wanted you to honor his memory? Is this how you keep the love you had for him alive?"

The girl stiffened, tears rolling down her cheeks as my question pierced her through the heart.

Candace shrank backward, blushing with embarrassment as the other kids at the choir table began shooting her dirty looks.

Belial was equally confused, baring his yellowed fangs in frustration. "What's the hold up?" he snarled. "Bash her head in already!"

Once again, that strange clarity brought something to the surface of my thoughts—Ethan's lecture about demonic weaknesses. I needed to pull Belial's attention away from Dani and focus it on me, and now I realized exactly how to do it. "What's wrong, Gordo? Can't tempt a 'pathetic' little human?"

"I told you to stop calling me that," the demon snapped. He glared over his shoulder at Diva, motioning to Candace. "What are you waiting for? Get over here and make your bully do her job! We gotta light a match between these brats!"

"Really? You need *help*?" I crossed one leg over the other, grinning smugly. "I thought you were the great and terrible lord of constipation or something. Since when did you have to beg your minions for assistance? Do you need someone to help strap on that leather diaper of yours?"

Belial slowly turned to face me. His voice plunged into a deep, monstrous growl, the pupils of his blood-red eyes narrowing into vertical slits. "Open your mouth...one more time..."

"And you'll what? Sic your concubines on me? Might as well. They've got more stones than you anyway."

That unleashed the kraken.

Belial exploded at me with a deafening roar, diving into a full-body tackle. I should've already drawn my swords, been standing in a defensive stance, but neither crossed my mind until the two of us were tumbling through the cafeteria windows.

We slipped seamlessly through the glass, through outdoor picnic tables and metal benches, landing in the center of the school courtyard. He made himself tangible and dug one of his hands into the ground, flinging me away as he came screeching to a halt, leaving a trail of claw marks behind him.

I went hurtling into the air, about to slam into the concrete when I remembered I wasn't bound by the laws of physics. Exerting an invisible force beneath me, I slowed my fall into a controlled backflip, skidding to a stop on my feet.

None of the students eating in the area realized they were now sitting in the middle of a warzone. They simply continued munching merrily under the shady trees and tarped overhangs, only a pair of mystified boys noticing Belial's gash in the floor. As for all the angels and demons present, they went scrambling to opposite sides of the courtyard, cautiously eyeing me and my adversary to get a bead on the situation. Some of the hellspawn inched toward me, eager to lend their aid to the Sin of Wrath, but fortunately my attack on his pride kept them at bay.

"Stay where you are," Belial barked at his kin. "This featherback is mine."

The other angels exchanged glances, wondering if they should get involved as well, but they quickly came to the same conclusion I did. We couldn't allow another free-for-all massacre like what happened with the food fight. This had to be a one-on-one. Just me and the fiendish Goliath.

"You wanna fight, perro?" I kicked off my sandals, my bare feet gliding over the cement as I crouched into an offensive stance. My twin scimitars materialized into my clenched hands, their curved blades extending to full length in a burst of white holy fire. "Ready when you are."

Belial smirked in amusement. "You've got guts, short stack. I'll give you that. I look forward to ripping them out through your neck." The demon stretched his arm to the side, silently calling to the shadows of the courtyard. They leapt from beneath the trees and benches into his open palm, coalescing to form a sphere of pure darkness. As he closed his fingers around it, the shadows narrowed into a hilt, fanning outward at the top to create a double-bladed axe. Its sweeping edges gleamed wickedly in the sunlight, black and hardened like obsidian, igniting in a shroud of purple hellfire. "Let's begin, shall we?"

I felt my skin tighten into goosebumps as he leveled the axe in my direction, immediately regretting my boldness. His spirit was exuding a completely different aura now. A burning, murderous intent, like an open furnace that almost smothered me where I stood. My every instinct screamed at me to run, to forfeit the challenge and save myself, but my legs couldn't seem to obey.

I blinked...and that alone nearly cost me everything.

Belial was already looming over me, having closed the distance between us with incredible speed. His axe swung down at my face, poised to split me in two, but I managed to deflect it with one of my swords at the last second, driving the other into his chest. Its tip bounced off his scaly gray skin as though he were made of solid stone, the shock of my ineffectiveness leaving me wide open.

"Nice try," he sneered. "My turn..."

Before I could react, the ball of his huge taloned foot slammed into my chest, launching me backward across the courtyard. The blow was so heavy it felt as if my whole rib cage was about to collapse, golden dust spewing from my mouth as I finally rolled to a stop.

"Why aren't you laughing?" Belial said mockingly. "You thought I was funny a minute ago. I guess *you* turned out to be the punchline."

I wiped the dust from my lips, leaning on my swords to pick myself up. "*Why?*" I panted. "Why us? Why Dani? There have to be more important souls out there for you to hunt. What did we ever do to deserve a cardinal diablo? There has to be a reason!"

"What did you do?" Belial tilted his head, his expression contorting with glee. "You mongrels were born, sweetheart. You chose light over darkness and sided with the Father, banishing Lucifer and the rest of my kind from Heaven. That's all the reason I need." He casually strode towards me, twirling the axe with his fingers. "Like I told you before, I couldn't care less who you people are, and I'll forget you right after I'm done. You're merely my next meal."

I grinded my teeth, righteous fury mounting inside me. "You're nothing but a tool for revenge."

"I am the Lord of Wrath!"

Belial shot forward, swiping his axe in a wide horizontal arc. Too afraid to block it, I willed myself intangible and quickly sank into the ground, vanishing out of sight as hardened shadow whizzed over my head.

"You can't hide forever, short stack." He slammed his axe down where I'd been a moment before, shattering the concrete beneath his feet. Broken shards flew into the air, startling the surrounding mortals.

"W-what was *that?*" one of them cried.

The demon turned, smashing another section of walkway.

"Is something falling from the sky?" another student yelled.

"Maybe it's an earthquake!"

Another crash sent them running in panic, Belial's impatience overriding discretion.

"I am the Vessel of Iniquity!" he roared, blowing apart the cement. "The Breaker of Souls!" He swung with two hands this time, splitting a fissure across the picnic area. "You're just a coward. Weak. Hypocritical. If you refuse to fight, then I'll simply finish what I started with your pitiful girl. Make her life miserable. Make her beg for death. Drag her to Hell like all the others I've tempted. Her screams will be absolutely music to my ears."

"I'll take your head first!"

I leapt out of the ground behind Belial, running up the back of his legs and torso with a flurry of lightning-quick slashes. None of them managed to break the skin, but I didn't care. I was a mother grizzly, and this ugly, oversized piece of gutter trash had dared to threaten my cub.

"That *girl* is my granddaughter!" I cried, slicing across the nape of his neck. "You don't know her! You don't love her! You wouldn't give your soul to protect hers!" The demon whirled around in time for both hilts to bash him in the forehead. "I'll send you back to Hell in a pile of ashes before I let you take her from me!"

Belial staggered backwards, clutching his face with a howl. Despite his incredibly tough hide, the blunt force of my last attack had actually done some damage. Unfortunately, it also succeeded in evoking his rage even further. He lunged forward, going for another explosive chop.

This time I was ready. The axe crashed into the ground, narrowly missing my sidestep, then, pinning it down with my foot, I swung my other leg high, driving my heel into Belial's jaw.

SNAP!

A jolt of pain shot up my leg, the bones in my foot fracturing under the weight of my blow. It felt like I'd just hammer-kicked an iron statue.

Belial grinned at me, completely unfazed. "Pathetic..." He buried his bowling ball of a fist in my gut, knocking the wind from my lungs.

I lurched backward, gasping for air, my vision blurry as he followed up with his newly freed axe. I tried to raise my swords, parry the strike, but its shadowy blade caught me in the shoulder, golden dust spraying from the wound as I toppled to the ground.

"It was fun while it lasted," the demon said, standing over me, blotting out the sun, "but it's time for you to come to an end." He raised the axe over his head with both hands, muscles rippling as he prepared to finish me.

I stared up at him, willing myself to move, but my angelic body had reached its limit. My broken foot throbbed in agony, dust trickling from my arm and mouth, everything trembling on the verge of surrender.

So I did the only thing I could.

I crossed my blades to meet his axe and offered a silent prayer.

Padre, I beg of you…please, help me.

Belial brought down his judgment with gritted teeth, sparks flying as hardened shadow clashed against celestial steel. My arms nearly buckled, somehow withstanding the impact, but the demon's crushing weight continued to press downward, slowly driving the edge of his weapon towards my face.

I was wrong…I can't do this alone. I never could. I never did, so please, give me the strength to repel this evil.

I waited, listening intently despite the burden of impending doom.

No answer came.

It already had.

While I'd been struggling in vain against Wrath, Dani had risen from her seat back in the cafeteria. Candace and the other students watched curiously as she snatched up her sack lunch, walking away from her nemesis without another word. She rounded the outer edge of the room, stopping next to a table with only a single patron.

Beth Starkovsky.

I noticed them through the windows now, the lone girl and her angel becoming overwhelmed with emotion as Dani asked if she could sit. Beth scooted over, smiling through the tears. Dani beamed in return, sliding down beside her, and for a fleeting moment, the rest of the room was totally still.

Then along came Hector. He hurried through Jezazel like she was a puff of black smoke, ignoring her cries as he went to join Dani. The choir kids got up as well, throwing Candace a few withering glares as they headed over. Before long, the table of two had been filled to the brim, the spirit of compassion made clear in the face of Candace's cruelty.

With her act of selflessness, Dani had unknowingly tipped the scales of power away from Belial, imbuing me with a strength I'd never felt before. The pain throughout my body faded to a dull ache, the axe bearing down on me becoming steadily lighter. I planted my uninjured foot on the ground, rising against my opponent's might.

He gasped, fear washing over him as my eyes began to glow white, my entire body erupting in a shroud of holy fire. "*What? How?* You aren't an arch-seraph! You're just another miserable featherback!"

"My name...is Sarai!" I thrust my twin blades apart with all the power I could muster, shattering Belial's axe into a million pieces.

He reeled backward, grimacing down at the dual slashes carved across his chest. The wounds smoldered with heat, deep enough to bleed some kind of inky black fluid, yet not quite enough to vanquish my foe.

"No...that's impossible," Belial said, looking up at me. "You were nothing a second ago. Where did...?" He trailed off as I pointed over his shoulder, directing his attention back to the cafeteria.

Several more kids and their angels had gathered around Dani, Hector and Beth, chatting excitedly with one another while Candace brooded alone in disbelief. The sheer positivity in the air was so strong that it sent the demons skulking to the far corners of the room.

A small group led by Diva and Jezazel went to accost the angels, their weapons at the ready, but Ethan stepped forward to meet them. White flames enveloped his body from head to toe, condensing around him to form his glittering, silvery armor. He summoned a sword and shield to finish the ensemble, banging them together loud enough for me to hear from outside.

Daunting as he was, Diva drew her whip anyway, its thorny coils snapping as she lashed it at the heavenly knight. He raised his enormous shield, easily shrugging off the blow. She tried again and again, not even leaving a mark on his heavy barrier. As she pulled back her arm for another attack, a second angel stepped forward, giving her pause.

It was Malachi. He strolled confidently up behind Ethan and placed a hand on his shoulder, acknowledging me through the window with a grateful nod. Then he closed his eyes and began to concentrate, a glowing aura surrounding him as he channeled his spiritual power into Ethan. Other angels quickly ran to join him, Ariel and Javan smiling at me as they added their strength to the pool.

Through the dark visor of Ethan's helmet, I could see his eyes burning bright like mine. His gilded broadsword lit up as well, its radiance blinding the demons, as though the sun itself had descended into the cafeteria. He raised it over his head, a beam of light shooting from the tip into the ceiling, then he brought it to his chest and swung it wide in front of him. The poor devils never stood a chance. Ethan's beam swept the room, disintegrating them all in an instant.

"*No...*" Belial took a step backward, gaping in horror at the ashes that were once Diva and Jezazel.

"Now then," I said, spinning my blades with a flourish, "where were we?"

He whirled around, eyes darting between me and the crowd of remaining demons lining the courtyard. Each of them stared right back, anxious to know what their esteemed leader would do next. With my battered body and busted foot, I wasn't entirely certain I could still win, but judging by the desperation on Belial's face, neither was he.

How would he ever live down the shame if he lost? Imagine the headline: One of the Seven Sins of Inferno dusted by a nobody. As long as I could hold my bluff, there was only one way for him to save his dignity.

"You bore me," he said, putting on a breezy facade. "Honestly, all you featherbacks and your theatrics over some teenage girl. What does it really matter who she stuffs her gullet with? I play the long game. She's got the whole rest of her life ahead of her. That's a lot of time to slip into the darkness, and I always win eventually."

"Why wait?" I taunted. "This was just getting fun."

"Love to disappoint, but I've got better things to do." Belial levitated into the air, beckoning to his demonic spectators. "Hey, who's up to party at the frat house around the corner? Drinks are on me!" His cohorts shrugged at each other, deciding to simply follow along. One by one, they drifted up and out of the courtyard, the Lord of Wrath muttering a final jab before retreating out of sight. "See ya after school, short stack."

I lingered motionless for a moment, letting the words roll off my back. Had they found me an hour ago, I probably would've been terrified, the ominous hint of punishment dogging the corners of my mind.

But not anymore.

I had a guardian of my own in Daniela. All this time, I'd coddled her, believing I was the only shield and sword, but she was the one who turned the tide. Her love and courage had saved me, and though the shadow of evil would inevitably return, things were different now. We'd face it together, stronger than ever before.

I exhaled deeply, relinquishing my swords in a burst of light. The shroud of flames around my body subsided, the glow fading from my eyes as I turned to the cafeteria windows. I couldn't hear them through the glass, but every angel inside was waving to me, jumping up and down with excitement. Ariel most of all. She was practically standing on top of Javan's head, arms flailing like a madwoman.

It made my cheeks heat up with embarrassment, but I was fine with that. Somehow, it helped take the sting out of my wounds. To avoid walking on my broken foot, I let myself float over the ground, passing through the windows on my way to the crowd. A blast of cheers and applause greeted me as I entered. Ariel sprinted ahead of the group, throwing herself at me for a bear hug.

"Sarai, that was amazing!" she said, cracking my back. "You actually beat a cardinal demon!"

"Ow ow ow! Ribs! Ribs!"

"Ooops...sorry..." Ariel pulled away, sheepishly brushing aside her long platinum hair. "I'm just so glad you're okay. After you insulted Belial's...um...manhood, we thought you were a goner."

"Now that you mention it, I guess I could've aimed a little lower with that last attack," I said, grinning at the mental image.

"You didn't have to," Javan said, strolling up beside us. "You made Wrath bleed. That's more than enough to change the way I look at this war." He glanced down at the floor, biting his lip. "I owe you an apology, Sarai. I never should've doubted—"

"You weren't the only one," I interjected. "I had no idea what all of you were capable of. We really are greater than the sum of our parts."

A metal glove reached out to softly pat me on the shoulder. "Wise words indeed." Ethan was still donning his full suit of armor, raising the visor from in front of his face to give me a wink. "The day is ours, Milady. Father's mercy be praised. Did you hear His guidance as well?"

I paused, thinking back on my moments of clarity before the battle. Though I hadn't heard a particular voice, there was an unmistakable presence. A peace and warmth I hadn't felt since the last time I'd set foot in Heaven all those years ago. Proof that I was never truly alone. "Yeah…I suppose I did."

"Bah! Where *are* my manners?" Ethan said, finally realizing I was covered in bruises. "A knight can't have his captain shambling around with untreated wounds."

"Wait, what? I'm a captain now?"

He clapped his hands, calling to a pair of nearby angels. "Healers! Come now, show the lady our appreciation!"

They jumped at his command without question, rushing over to address my heel and shoulder. I recoiled slightly, opening my mouth to rebuke Ethan for conscripting them, but quickly surrendered to their soothing touch. Their hands illuminated in the same way as Laila's, replacing my damaged tissue with tingling perfection.

"What say you?" Ethan asked, grinning with approval. "Not bad for a captain's welcome, is it?"

"I could get used to it," I mumbled, eyes blissfully rolling back in my head.

"It would seem I am in thy debt yet again." Malachi stepped out from behind Ethan, regarding me with a hallowed reverence. "At last, Beth has someone here to call friend. Never have I seen her so happy."

I peered over his shoulder at the clamoring table of students, watching as they talked and laughed. Hector had grabbed a couple of corn dogs, using them as makeshift drumsticks to entertain Beth and the others. And Dani. I could've melted on the spot with the smile on her face. There was no longer a trace of pain or sorrow. No loneliness or regret. She wasn't even the girl I knew from the first day of school. She'd become something else. Something greater. What her papa had always hoped she would be—a child of light.

"I'm not the one to thank," I told Malachi. "I didn't do a thing. Turning away from anger? Putting aside the judgment of others? That was all Dani."

"But to resist Belial..."

I shook my head. "What about you? You stood against the rest of the demons with Tin Man over here. You set an example of courage and unity for the other angels to follow. *I* should be thanking *you*."

Malachi blushed, his pale cheeks turning the same shade as his freckles. "So, what now?" he asked. "The devils are bound to return eventually, are they not?"

"Sooner or later."

"And Belial? He still dwells among us. Art thou not fearful he will one day overcome thee?"

I flexed my newly healed arm and leg, smiling at my granddaughter as she pulled my necklace from her shirt and kissed the pendant. "He's more than welcome to try."

Did you enjoy the story?

If so, please leave a review for the book on Amazon! It doesn't have to be anything long or fancy, but every single review is incredibly valuable to an author and helps get their stories out into the world!

For more updates on the *Gray Spirits* series, be sure to join my quarterly newsletter by scanning the QR code below. You'll also get access to future beta reading opportunities, short stories, and plenty of other exclusive content!

Newsletter Sign Up

Acknowledgments

My first thanks will always be to my Heavenly Father and Jesus Christ. It is only through their love, encouragement and inspiration that I'm able to put these crazy ideas of mine onto paper. Science fiction was the catalyst that spurred me into storytelling, however, the *Gray Spirits* series, especially the next book, *Memoirs of a Household Demon*, holds a special place in my heart because of how much closer to home it feels. The message of hope and faith is real, and I pray my readers are able to walk away from my stories with a renewed sense of purpose and self-worth.

I'm so grateful for my family: My wife, Valerie, Mom, Dad, Stephanie and Don as well as my in-laws, Jacob and Diane. All of you have been my greatest cheerleaders and your input has kept my sanity in check more times than I can count. I can never thank you enough for being my guinea pigs and my stories would never be what they are without you. Thanks for always believing in me even when I couldn't find the strength to do it myself.

Thank you to all my beta readers, Mary Locke Jolley, Kayla MacNeille, Diane Taylor, Don Logsdon and Stephanie Jerdon. Your energy and enthusiasm for my characters is the wind beneath my wings. I loved hearing your feedback, and your attention to detail has been a lifesaver.

Thank you to Carmella Grace for the amazing book cover and chapter heading artwork. It's been a joy to see your talents give this story new life.

Last, but certainly not least, thank you to my readers! So many of you have reached out and expressed your love for this story and its characters. You've laughed, cried and cheered for them, and sharing that experience with you is what makes the countless hours in front my keyboard some of the best spent of my life. I look forward to meeting more of you in the future, and to those of you thirsty for more of the *Gray Spirits* universe, rest easy. There's plenty of goodies yet to come.

About The Author

Ben Logsdon grew up in Yucaipa, California, where he learned the subtle charm of small towns and nerd culture. He's been a saxophone player, a driving instructor, a sci-fi connoisseur, a mechanical engineer and also a lover of cocktail shrimp. After serving a Christian mission to the country of Panama, he picked up Spanish and developed a penchant for storytelling. Since then, he's started a writing platform (Red Nova Books, @rednovabooks) and authored multiple books in the genres of urban fantasy and science fiction. Ben enjoys playing tennis, watching anime and keeping up with the latest video games. If he isn't spending time with his wife and three kids, he's probably out back pitching ideas to his adopted Calico cat.

For more updates on the *Gray Spirits* series and Ben's other books, be sure to check out his website:

www.rednovabooks.com

Milton Keynes UK
Ingram Content Group UK Ltd.
UKHW031355011224
451755UK00004B/303